Welcome to

Nestled on the rugged Cor[nish coast lies the] town of Penhally. With [... stunning] landscapes and a warm, bustling community—it is the lucky tourist who stumbles upon this little haven.

But now Mills & Boon® Medical™ Romance is giving readers the unique opportunity to visit this fictional coastal town through our brand-new twelve-book continuity… You are welcomed to a town where the fishing boats bob up and down in the bay, surfers wait expectantly for the waves, friendly faces line the cobbled streets and romance flutters on the Cornish sea breeze…

We introduce you to Penhally Bay Surgery, where you can meet the team led by caring and commanding Dr Nick Tremayne. Each book will bring you an emotional, tempting romance—from Mediterranean heroes to a sheikh with a guarded heart. There's royal scandal that leads to marriage for a baby's sake, and handsome playboys are tamed by their blushing brides! Top-notch city surgeons win adoring smiles from the community, and little miracle babies will warm your hearts. But that's not all...

With Penhally Bay you get double the reading pleasure… as each book also follows the life of damaged hero Dr Nick Tremayne. His story will pierce your heart—a tale of lost love and the torment of forbidden romance. Dr Nick's unquestionable, unrelenting skill would leave any patient happy in the knowledge that she's in safe hands, and is a testament to the ability and dedication of all the staff at Penhally Bay Surgery. Come in and meet them for yourself…

Dear Reader

I live in a house that overlooks the sea. Half a mile from my study window I can see oil tankers, cargo vessels, ferries and cruise ships, sailing between green and red buoys, making their way up-channel to dock in Liverpool. I spend too much time gazing out to sea, wondering where the ships have been, where they are going. I wonder what stories they could tell.

A trip on a cruise ship is an escape. For a while you are insulated from the real world, pampered and cosseted. In this book Maddy and Ed are trying to escape their pasts—if in different ways. It takes an epidemic on board ship to show them that the best way to escape is not to run, but to face your demons. Both must seize the love that they thought would never come their way again.

Best wishes

Gill

NURSE BRIDE, BAYSIDE WEDDING

BY
GILL SANDERSON

MILLS & BOON®

Pure reading pleasure

**To my midwife daughter, Helen, who has
helped me so much.**

First published in Great Britain 2008
Harlequin Mills & Boon Limited,
Eton House, 18-24 Paradise Road, Richmond, Surrey TW9 1SR

© Gill Sanderson 2008

ISBN: 978 0 263 86320 8

Set in Times Roman 10½ on 12¾ pt
03-0508-50643

Printed and bound in Spain
by Litografia Rosés, S.A., Barcelona

Gill Sanderson, aka Roger Sanderson, started writing as a husband-and-wife team. At first Gill created the storyline, characters and background, asking Roger to help with the actual writing. But her job became more and more time-consuming, and he took over all of the work. He loves it!

Roger has written many Medical™ Romance books for Harlequin Mills & Boon. Ideas come from three of his children—Helen is a midwife, Adam a health visitor, Mark a consultant oncologist. Weekdays are for work; weekends find Roger walking in the Lake District or Wales.

Recent titles by the same author:

THEIR MIRACLE CHILD
A BABY OF THEIR OWN
THE DOCTOR'S BABY SURPRISE
A SURGEON, A MIDWIFE: A FAMILY

BRIDES OF PENHALLY BAY

*Bachelor doctors become husbands and fathers—
in a place where hearts are made whole.*

**At Christmas pregnant Lucy Tremayne
was reunited with the man she loved**
Christmas Eve Baby by Caroline Anderson

We snuggled up in January with gorgeous Italian, Dr Avanti
The Italian's New-Year Marriage Wish by Sarah Morgan

Romance blossomed for Adam and Maggie in February
The Doctor's Bride By Sunrise by Josie Metcalfe

**Single dad Jack Tremayne found
his perfect bride in March**
The Surgeon's Fatherhood Surprise by Jennifer Taylor

In April a princess arrived in Penhally!
The Doctor's Royal Love-Child by Kate Hardy

This May Edward Tremayne finds the woman of his dreams
Nurse Bride, Bayside Wedding by Gill Sanderson

**Gorgeous Chief Inspector Lachlan D'Ancey
is married in June**
Single Dad Seeks a Wife by Melanie Milburne

**The temperature really hots up in August—
Dr Oliver Fawkner arrives in the Bay…**
Virgin Midwife, Playboy Doctor by Margaret McDonagh

**In August Francesca and Mike try one last time
for the baby they've longed for**
Their Miracle Baby by Caroline Anderson

**September brings sexy Sheikh Zayed
to the beaches of Penhally**
Sheikh Surgeon Claims His Bride by Josie Metcalfe

Snuggle up with dishy Dr Tom Cornish in October
A Baby for Eve by Maggie Kingsley

**And don't miss French doctor Gabriel,
who sweeps into the Bay this November**
Dr Devereux's Proposal by Margaret McDonagh

A collection to treasure for ever!

CHAPTER ONE

'WILL you marry me, Maddy? We'll live in my big white house on the hill and have strawberries for breakfast every morning.'

Nurse Madeleine Granger smiled. 'Sounds a good idea, especially the strawberries. I'd love to marry you, Mr Bryce, but people might say I was after your money.'

'It's my money, I can do what I want with it. And I'd do anything to stop the Chancellor of the Exchequer getting it all. Ow!'

'I'm sorry. I know it hurts, but…'

'It doesn't matter. My fault for tripping up the stairs and scratching my leg.'

'This was more than a scratch. I've been treating it for ten days now—and it's only just starting to heal.' Maddy dusted antiseptic powder over the ulcerated shin, then reached for a dressing. Sometimes old people's wounds took a long time to heal, especially when there was little flesh between skin and bone. And Malcolm Bryce was an eighty-five-year-old widower. But he was alert, sprightly and had made more new friends than anyone else on the ship.

'So you won't marry me? I'm going to be terribly disappointed.' She loved the mischievous sparkle in his eyes when he teased her.

'I'd certainly marry you if I wanted to marry anyone. But I don't. For me marriage is out. O-U-T.'

There was a keenness in his faded eyes. 'You seem very certain of that.'

'I am.' Her reply was gentle, but firm.

'Ah, well. Rebuffed again. But I will be strong. So what should I do with the Bryce millions?'

'Spend them. Come for another cruise to the Indian Ocean on the good ship *Emerald*.'

'Well, I have enjoyed it. Didn't you say it was your first trip as a cruise-ship nurse? Have you enjoyed it?'

Maddy smiled. 'It's a lot more luxurious than the hospital A and E department I came from. Yes, I have enjoyed it, I've made a lot of new friends. Now, for the past few days you've come to the medical centre for treatment. But today you phoned and asked me to come to your cabin. Any special reason why?'

In fact, she had noticed that he didn't look his usual healthy self. He was still lying in his bed, unknown for him at this time of day. He was pale, there were beads of sweat on his forehead. Although he tried to keep up their normal cheerful chatter, his voice was noticeably weaker.

'I feel a bit feeble,' he said. 'When I woke up this morning my left arm was numb and tingly. Then I went back to sleep again and I never do that.'

'Did you have palpitations? Could you feel your heart beating harder than usual?'

Mr Bryce considered. 'Sort of,' he said. 'It seemed queer—irregular. But I still went back to sleep.'

Maddy tried not to show the concern she was feeling. 'You're probably a bit excited at the prospect of getting back home,' she said. 'It affects some people that way. Still, I'll check your blood pressure and listen to your heart.'

His BP was too high and his heartbeat seemed unsteady. Well, he was a man of eighty-five but… 'I think you'd better stay in bed today,' she said. 'In fact, you might as well stay in bed till we dock. Then I'll get a doctor to come and look at you. I'll get a steward to fetch you your meals—nothing heavy and no alcohol. And I think I'll prescribe aspirin as well.'

Mr Bryce nodded. 'I've had a minor stroke, haven't I, Maddy? A transient ischaemic attack.'

'What do you know about transient ischaemic attacks?' Maddy was shocked at the way he guessed what she was thinking.

'A temporary reduction of blood and oxygen to the brain, probably caused by a minor blood clot. My wife had several of them before she died and I got to recognise the symptoms. But mostly, Maddy, I'm upset because you won't marry me.' The smile was still there but the voice was getting weaker.

'Perhaps I'll think about it,' she said gently. 'Now, rest. The steward will come to see to you and I'll drop in again later.'

'Looking forward to that,' said Mr Bryce.

Maddy's next call was two decks further up. Another phone call asking for a cabin visit. It was unusual as most people much preferred to come to the medical centre. Maddy's suspicions were growing. She knocked, and a weak voice asked her to come in.

Entering the cabin, the smell was unmistakable, and a glance at the white-faced patient confirmed that Mrs Adams was feeling very unwell indeed. Maddy's heart sank as she realised what she could be dealing with. This wasn't the first stomach upset she'd treated in the last twenty-four hours. 'How are you feeling, Mrs Adams?'

'Nurse, I feel like I'm dying. I've been sick and I…I don't think I can get out of bed.'

'Well, let's take your temperature for a start. And we'll check your pulse and BP. When did you start to feel ill?'

'It happened so suddenly! I didn't much feel like my meal last night. I thought I'd be better in the morning, but in the middle of the night I…' And Mrs Adams was sick again.

Reassuring the poor woman, who kept apologising weakly, Maddy cleaned her up and made her as comfortable as possible. 'There you go, Mrs Adams, and you're to stay in bed all day. Whatever you do, don't leave your cabin. Don't try to eat anything, but if you can, drink plenty. I've got some special stuff here. No tap water and especially nothing sweet. And take these pills now. I'll put a couple of bottles near you. And I'll be in to see you later.'

'I don't think I've ever felt as bad as this in my life,' Mrs Adams whispered.

'We'll do what we can to get you better. Now, just rest.' Maddy wondered if she looked as confident as she sounded.

She walked back to the medical centre, washed her hands again, made herself a coffee and sat down to think. Late last night it had been just a vague suspicion, but now it was turning into a certainty. This was going to be trouble. And it could be big trouble.

There had been plenty to occupy her during the cruise. Many of the passengers were quite elderly and had the usual ailments that come with age. But mostly it had been small stuff. The medical staff had coped easily.

And until yesterday morning she had been just one member of a medical team—the least important member. There had been a doctor on board, and another nurse. But a launch had met them as they'd approached the British coast, taking off the doctor and the other nurse. There had been an illness, and the doctor and nurse were needed urgently on a cruise ship about to depart. And since the *Emerald* was practically in British coastal waters, due to dock in two days, it had been decided that one nurse would be sufficient.

She now thought that was doubtful.

Last night there had been two complaints about upset stomachs. This morning she had treated another person—and it looked like there would be more. In an enclosed environment like a cruise ship, illness could spread like wildfire.

She winced. She thought that these were cases of acute gastroenteritis, sometimes known as cruise ship fever.

It was important that the captain be informed at once—he had to make the big decisions. But to a certain extent he'd have to rely on her medical advice. She knew he'd be fair—but he wouldn't be happy.

Especially when she told him that the port authorities might not let them dock.

She picked up her phone and told Ken Jackson, the captain's steward, that she needed to see the captain urgently.

'Urgently?' Ken asked. 'He is pretty busy now, arranging docking, and—'

'Ken, I said urgently and I meant it.'

He caught her tone. 'I'll ring you back,' he said.

She sat down to wait, to get her thoughts in order. Captain Smith would want precision. She'd give it to him.

In fact, she only had to wait five minutes before the phone rang. She picked it up at once. 'Captain Smith, I—'

'Hello, Maddy? Have you missed me?'

She had been expecting to hear from the captain and this was not his voice. She knew she recognised it but who could…? And then she realised and stiffened with horror. It was a voice she had never wanted to hear again.

It was Brian Temple, her ex-fiancé…the cause of so much pain. It was the man who was responsible for her giving up the A and E work she had enjoyed so much. The man who had ruined her life. The man responsible for her taking on this job—just to get away from him.

'Are you there, Maddy? I know it's you.' There was that faint alteration in tone. Brian always needed attention at once.

'What do you want, Brian? I thought I made it quite clear I never wanted to hear from you again. You seemed to get the message, to accept it. We agreed that everything between us was over.'

As ever, he paid no attention to what he didn't want to hear. 'You know you didn't mean that. A pal of yours told me that you were docking tomorrow, so I thought I might meet you off the ship. We could get together and go and have a chat and a drink.'

'No! We've been through all that. Brian, we are over!'

His voice took on that whining, angry tone that she

knew so well and hated so much. 'Maddy, I love you! We love each other, we both know that.'

'We don't love each other. I'm not seeing you, Brian. I wish you well but you're out of my life for ever.'

'You can't say that!'

She could feel genuine pain in his voice so gently she asked, 'Are you taking your medication regularly?'

'I don't need it so I stopped.'

Maddy sighed. This was likely to go on for ever.

He paused a moment and his voice took on a totally different, more unpleasant tone. 'I suppose you've found somebody else. A fancy ship's officer or some rich old man. Well, I told you before, I won't have it.'

Suspicion. Was there anything more hateful than constant, unprovoked suspicion? Their entire relationship had been tormented by it. For a moment she was angry, and was tempted to lie to him, to tell him that she had indeed met a man. But she knew better. It would only cause more trouble.

'After you, I never want to meet another man,' she said. 'Now, don't ever ring me again.'

But she knew as she replaced the receiver that it was a forlorn hope.

She went into her cabin and took out the folder of personal papers in the bottom drawer of her desk. For some reason she had kept the last message Brian had sent her when she had set off on the cruise ship. She reread it— it was half pleading, half threatening. And he reminded her of the good times they had had.

She supposed there had been some good times. Trips to the coast. A weekend in London. Meals she had cooked for him. And their plans for the future—she wanted at least two babies. But then it had all gone bad. She had been unlucky in love—always. Every time she had met a man something had gone wrong.

She took a couple of deep breaths to calm herself. She looked out of the porthole, trying to take some comfort from the English coastline she could see slipping past. It looked beautiful in the sun but she was not glad to be back in Britain. There were going to be problems. The terror was coming back.

She could see cliffs, green moors behind them, the odd white-painted or grey stone cottage. Four years ago she had worked here as a practice nurse for a summer. She'd worked for a Dr Tremayne—Nick Tremayne. He'd been a good doctor. They still exchanged Christmas cards but that was all. In one card he'd told her that he'd moved to a village in Cornwall called Penhally Bay. It must be around here somewhere. She hoped he was happy. Somebody ought to be.

Her phone rang again and she looked at it apprehensively. It might be Brian…but it was Ken Jackson. 'Could you come up to see the captain now, please, Maddy?'

She glanced in the mirror, made sure her shoulder-length hair was tied back, her uniform neat. Captain Smith was very keen on tidiness. 'Untidy dress suggests an untidy mind which suggests untidy work,' he had told her. 'That's how I run my ship.' She liked him for it.

She took a deep breath, picked up her case notes and walked up to his cabin.

Captain Smith was a giant, white-bearded man. Maddy knew he'd had a distinguished career in the Royal Navy—

on the walls of his cabin there were photographs of the ships he had commanded. He smiled at her, invited her to sit down. 'You need to see me urgently, Maddy?'

This was a job she didn't want. She had never dealt with anything like this before. Most of her nursing career had been in A and E rather than dealing with infectious diseases. But, still, it was her duty to report what she suspected.

'I think we may have an outbreak of an infectious disease,' she said. 'Exactly what I don't know, but it seems to be gastroenteritis. You might think it necessary to inform the port authorities. And they might want to quarantine the ship.'

Captain Smith kept his emotions under strict control. But Maddy could see how much this news dismayed him. Still, he wasn't going to panic. 'I see. How many cases so far?'

'Four. But this kind of thing spreads very rapidly. I suspect there'll be more as soon as I get back to the medical centre.'

'I can believe it. You know that gastroenteritis is sometimes known as the cruise ship disease?'

'I've heard it called that.'

Captain Smith thought for a moment. 'And you are the only medical staff I have.'

'Quite a few of the stewards have a little medical training. I have a list of them. They are a willing crew and they could act as orderlies. But that is all.'

'True. But we lost a doctor and a nurse yesterday.'

Maddy could see that had angered him, but he was not going to say so.

'Just how serious is this outbreak?'

It was necessary here for her to be absolutely accurate. 'I'm not an expert. But I do know that gastroenteritis can vary tremendously in seriousness. And because many of our passengers are old, they'll be particularly vulnerable. To find what has caused it, we need someone who can carry out laboratory investigations. I doubt there'll be any deaths but it will be extremely unpleasant. And, quite frankly, although I feel quite competent to deal with the condition, I need more professional help. There could be just too many cases.'

'I can see that. And when I find out who authorised the removal of two-thirds of my medical team…' The captain looked thoughtful. 'Of course, we have to report this to the port authorities and they'll not let us dock until we know more about the situation. I'll be in touch with our head office, but they tend not to move too fast in cases like this. So this is my problem.'

'I have a suggestion,' Maddy said hesitantly, 'if you don't mind.'

'I don't mind. If you can be of help, that is fine by me.'

'There's a doctor I used to work with who lives on the Cornish Coast near here. If he's available, he'd come out. And I know he's quite an expert in his field. He might give you the advice you need. His name is Nick Tremayne. Tell him I'm the nurse here.'

'Telephone number?'

Maddy shrugged. 'I only know that he has a surgery in Penhally Bay.'

Captain Smith took up his phone. 'Jackson? There's a Dr Tremayne who works in Penhally Bay, which is a few miles away. See if you can get him on the phone.'

Surprisingly quickly, the phone rang back. 'Dr Nick Tremayne? I'm Captain Smith, captain of the large ship you might see a couple of miles off shore. We have a medical problem.'

Unashamedly, Maddy listened in to the conversation. 'Recommended by a Nurse Madeleine Granger…suspected outbreak of gastroenteritis. This would be a private consultation… So quickly? I'd be much obliged.'

He turned to Maddy. 'Your doctor's coming out at once. He says that perhaps I don't understand how quickly this can spread to become an epidemic. But I do.'

Dr Ed Tremayne always rose early. He never slept very much. Those early morning half-sleeps, when you weren't sure of what was real and what was imagined. Or remembered. And then you woke to reality. It made you vulnerable and Ed didn't like feeling vulnerable. He liked to feel he was in control.

For England at the beginning of May, it was a very hot early morning. And it was close too, not like the dry blast of African heat that he remembered so well.

He parked his car by the beach, kicked off his trainers and tracksuit. Most days he came to this little cove for his early morning swim. He loved it. He loved the solitude and he liked the feeling of freedom in the water.

He stretched, then carefully looked round him. An old habit that he couldn't lose. He liked to know where he was, if there was anything he ought to be aware of. There were thick clouds on the horizon, and his experienced eye told him that there would be bad weather later in the day. He also saw a small tent half-hidden in the bushes. In summer a lot of young people came down here, sleeping wherever they could.

He ran to the sea, glad that no one was around. They'd stare, not at his well-muscled body, but at the scars.

He swam straight out of the cove mouth. He swam hard and fast, there was pleasure in pushing himself. And when he was in the open sea he stopped, trod water for a moment and again looked around him. Then he frowned.

A hundred yards away there was a rubber dinghy holding two young people, aged seventeen or eighteen, splashing, enjoying themselves, with two tiny paddles. Ed trod water nearby.

'I don't think you know these waters,' he warned. 'There's a rip tide out there and if you get caught in it you'll be pulled out to sea. Better get back into the cove. You'll be safe there.'

'We know what we're doing,' the lad said. 'We'll get back when we're good and ready.'

'I do suggest you go back now,' Ed said quietly. 'I know these waters. We have a few people drown every year. You want to be one of them?'

'Yeah, drownings, right. Tell you what, you be careful you don't drown yourself. At least we've got some kind of boat.'

Ed swam closer. 'Paddle this thing back into the cove,' he said mildly, 'or I'll turn it over and you can swim back.'

'You'll kill us!'

Ed's voice was calm but firm. 'I'm trying to stop you from killing yourselves.'

Suddenly the girl spoke. 'Kieran, he might be right. And I'm fed up with being out here anyway.' She looked at Ed. 'We're going back now.'

'I'll hang around until I see you in the cove.'

He thought he saw that the lad might still be willing to argue, so he said, still in a calm voice, 'See that shelf of rock over there?'

The two looked to where he was pointing. 'Yeah.'

'We found a drowned tourist there two years ago. He'd been in the water two days. He wasn't a pleasant sight. Now, start paddling back.'

They did. They paddled hard.

Ed finished his swim and when he got back into the cove he discovered that the couple, the rubber dinghy and the tent had gone. He shrugged. He knew he'd been hard on them. But better to lose face than be dead.

He looked round again. On the horizon he saw a cruise ship—not a big one. And close behind it were the dark clouds that meant a storm was coming.

CHAPTER TWO

HE'D only just bought his cottage. Was still working on it slowly, trying to decide what sort of home he needed. Which meant, of course, what sort of life he wanted to lead. So the cottage seemed somehow half-finished.

He'd never owned a house before so he loved it. And he knew that in time he'd turn it into the kind of home he would love even more. But something was missing. He knew what it was but he wouldn't let himself dwell on it. He had made plans, but those plans had been wrecked. Now he had to go forward; the past was gone.

He had a shower, a quick breakfast and drove up to the surgery. He was not yet a proper partner in the practice, but his father was anxious that he should join them as quickly as possible. There was plenty of work.

Officially, he was still on sick leave after leaving the army. But that would soon be over. Anyway, he felt well. More or less.

He loved the work of being a GP, loved the variety, the chance to meet and to know his patients. But in that case…why was he not more happy than he was? He shook his head, angry with himself. Troubles were there to be overcome.

He was early at the surgery as usual. He walked to the staff lounge. The door was open and there was Nick, his father, talking cheerfully to Kate Althorp, a midwife at the practice. It wasn't like his father to look so relaxed. His head was bent low over some papers on the table and Kate's head was close to his. The two were laughing at something.

Just a bit odd, Ed thought. There seemed to be a togetherness there that he hadn't noticed before. Then he decided he was imagining things.

They hadn't heard him arrive so for a minute Ed stood and looked at them. His father was a tall, lean, imposing figure, made more imposing by his habitual reserve. He tended to command instant respect—but not instant love. Ed had seen little of his father in recent years, and had never really been close to him. As a man he was hard to get through to. But Ed was trying. The trouble was, they were both reserved men.

He coughed, feeling almost like an intruder. Both looked up and smiled. Kate's was the friendly warm smile that made everyone take to her. His father's smile was, well, genuine, but cautious.

'You're early, aren't you?' Nick asked. 'And I thought you didn't have surgery this morning.'

'I don't. I'm going up to Clintons' farm. I want to see Isaac Clinton and I called in to check through his notes.'

His father was interested. 'Are there problems?'

'I don't think it's anything too serious—not yet. His daughter phoned last night, and asked me to call some time today. She thought her father might have had another angina attack in the afternoon, but she persuaded him to lie down and it passed.'

Kate collected the papers on the table and stuffed them into her briefcase. 'I think we've finished here, Nick, and I've got things to do. I'll leave you two to talk business. Bye, Ed.' Another happy smile and she was gone.

Nick looked after her for a while. Ed wondered what he was thinking. It was not like his father to be pensive so early in the morning. But then Nick shook himself and said, 'Isaac Clinton is an awkward old so-and-so. He thinks that farm will fall to bits if he isn't always on the lookout. And he's got a great farm manager in Ellie, that daughter of his. Would you like me to—'

'My patient,' Ed interrupted. 'There's no need for you to bother. I'll talk some sense into him. I promise you, if I need help I'll ask for it.'

'Of course, of course. I've got every confidence in you. You know before his heart attack Isaac had a history of injuries? I spent no end of time up there sewing him together. He just wasn't safe anywhere near farm machinery. Good farmer, though.'

'I've looked through his notes,' Ed said with a grin. 'If he'd got that many injuries in the army, he'd have had a dozen medals by now.'

His father smiled back. 'And I'll bet when you first met him he told you about every injury?'

'In great detail.'

Conversation between them was easier now they were discussing medicine, but it had always been like this. They avoided talking about feelings and there was seldom any obvious show of affection. Personal relationships, espe-

GILL SANDERSON 23

cially with those they loved, just weren't their best point. Even though they both tried. Ed suspected that the feelings were there, they were just never shown. He felt it was a pity.

He drove high onto the moors, enjoying the sunshine. But the air was still close; there was an unpleasant stickiness to it. He knew that some time soon there'd be a storm. Everyone in Penhally kept an eye on the weather.

Clintons' farm was well kept. Ed drove into the farmyard and was met at the farmhouse front door by Ellie Clinton. She must have been looking out for him. She smiled, a smile of welcome rather than relief—obviously she was not too worried about her father. Ed had met her several times before. Even though she was the farm manager, she always seemed to be around when he called to see Isaac.

'Dr Tremayne, it's good to see you. You must be warm—can I get you a glass of lemonade? I made it myself. Or tea or coffee?'

'Nothing, thanks. How is your father?'

Ellie stood back from the door, waving him inside. 'Well, you know. He's as awkward as ever. Yesterday I caught him loading stones into a cart, he looked dreadful. After an argument I got him to go to bed. And I phoned you. Are you sure you wouldn't like some lemonade?'

He knew it was probably the wrong thing to do. He wanted the relationship with Ellie to remain strictly doctor-patient, not hostess-guest. But it was hot and she obviously wanted him to try some. 'Perhaps a small glass,' he said. 'Thanks, Ellie.'

He was a guest now so he had to sit down to drink his lemonade and make conversation. He looked at Ellie. She was definitely very attractive, dressed today in a sleeveless, rather low-cut blue dress. She was wearing more obvious lipstick, her hair freshly washed and gleaming. A bit different from the usual farmer's boots, jeans and T-shirt. 'Going out somewhere?' he asked.

She did a little pirouette, the skirt swirling round her calves. 'Do you like the dress? It was such a lovely day, and I had to wait in for you, so I thought I'd try it on. It's new, I bought it for the hospital benefit ball. It's next Saturday. You know, St Piran Hospital. You are going, aren't you?'

Ed frowned. 'Somebody mentioned something about it at the surgery. I think quite a few of them are going but I'm not.'

'But you must! It's a very good cause, they're trying to buy a new scanner. And if the doctors can't support it, well, that's a pity.'

She looked at him, elaborately casually, as if she had just thought of something. 'In fact, I have a spare ticket. I was going with my cousin but she can't make it. You could go as my guest if you liked. The hospital has done a lot for Dad, I'd like to pay a bit back.'

For a moment Ed was tempted. Ellie was an attractive woman, intelligent, and had a great sense of humour. Any man would enjoy her company and be proud to be seen with her. But…why start something that he knew could never have a happy ending? He shook his head, smiled and said, 'It's just not my thing. I don't like big parties. But I approve of the scanner so I'll buy a book of raffle tickets at the surgery. Now, tell me about your father.'

Ellie smiled sadly and said, 'He's not been too bad today. He's waiting in his room to see you. Do you want to go up?'

Isaac was sitting by the window in his bedroom. He looked up as Ed entered and said, 'I'm all right, there's nothing wrong with me. That daughter of mine—'

'Is too good for you. She's concerned about you and by the look of you, she has cause to be. Now, do you want to lie on that bed and let me have a look at you?'

Just the usual examination. At first Isaac seemed reasonably healthy, but when Ed eventually listened to his heart he didn't like the murmurs he could hear.

'Are you taking your pills regularly, Isaac?'

'Well, yes, more or less, but they don't seem to do much for me. I don't feel any better for taking them.'

'They do plenty for you. And they're not meant to make you feel better. They're to ensure that you don't get any worse. Listen, Isaac, it's hard to take but you have to face up to it. You're not the man you used to be. You can't be, you're getting old. And that happens to all of us. You go out into that farmyard of yours again, pretend that you're a man of thirty instead of sixty-six and one day…'

'I'll be ready for the knacker's yard,' Isaac said with relish. 'Don't wrap things up nicely do you, Doctor?'

'You don't need nice, Isaac, you need truth. Now, we're not stopping you from taking a gentle walk around the place, keeping an eye on things. I've told you exactly what you can and what you can't do. And keep taking the pills regularly!'

Ed nodded at the view across the fields that Isaac had been surveying. 'You would miss this place if you had to spend months in a nursing home, wouldn't you?'

It was hard but it was necessary if he was going to get through to this stubborn old farmer. 'Could it be that bad?' Isaac asked. He was obviously shaken by that, if nothing else.

Ed patted him on the shoulders. 'We don't want to find out,' he said.

There was a tap at the door. Ellie came in with a jug of lemonade and two glasses. 'Have you talked sense into him?' she asked. But there was an obviously fond look at her father.

Ed smiled. 'He's got you to keep an eye on him,' he said. 'So he should be all right. Now, Isaac, you're to keep to the house for the next three days. No further than the front door. Plenty of bed rest. Then take it easy, a step at a time after that. Ellie, if there's any change you can ring me at any time, OK?'

'OK,' she said. And added hopefully, 'Are you sure I can't persuade you about the ticket?'

'It's just not my thing,' he repeated. He saw the disappointment in her eyes.

Driving back to Penhally, he wondered why he had turned Ellie down. He doubted if there was an unattached woman as attractive as her anywhere in the little town. And he had been attracted. So why had he refused her invitation?

Partly, he knew, it was because he wanted to be fair to her. He knew he could never give her what she wanted. A purely physical relationship, that was fine—but she deserved more than that. He knew the closeness she wanted, because once he had had it himself. He had lost it. And he was not going to risk more pain by looking for it again.

* * *

When Ed got out of his car to walk into the surgery he found his shirt sticking to his back. He'd already discarded his tie and jacket. Even moving slowly was like wading through warm water. He looked up at the grey skies and frowned.

As he walked past the reception desk his father came to the door of his room, phone clasped to his ear. He waved at Ed to come and join him. After Ed entered the room, his father promptly shut the door behind him. Ed heard him say, 'OK, Captain, you sort things out with your head office. I'll make arrangements to come out to you at once… No, I can do it quicker myself… Fine, we'll call it a private call.'

He put down the phone, looked at Ed and said, 'There's an emergency. There's a cruise ship just off shore and they need a doctor.'

'I thought all cruise ships had doctors.'

'They did have one. He was taken off the ship yesterday. And now they need him more than ever.'

'Always the way,' said Ed. 'What's the problem?'

'A virus—it's spreading like mad, turning into an epidemic.'

Ed was aware that his father was studying him, and he knew why. But he managed to keep his neutral expression and said nothing.

His father went on, 'It's gastroenteritis, but we've no idea what has caused it. Could be mild, it could be severe.'

There was a moment's pause and then Ed said, 'Well, I'm available this afternoon, and I'm the obvious one to go.'

He knew what his father was going to say next, but he waited for him to say it.

'I think I ought to go,' Nick said after a while. 'I know

the nurse who's reporting it, we've worked well together in the past. She thinks it might be quite serious.'

'But you've got surgery all afternoon and this evening. I'm available.' Ed paused a minute and then said, 'Come on, Dad, I know what you're thinking. So say it.'

Nick smiled, though it wasn't a very happy smile. 'Don't have much time for the niceties, do you? But I appreciate it. All right, I'm not sure you're fit to deal with a possible large-scale infection. It will bring back memories.'

'But I am the man who has dealt with an epidemic. In this case, I'm the expert. I know you're the best man to do the lab work, to work out what strain it is. But for the hour-to-hour medical care, the general organisation, I'm the best. And I can cope with my memories.'

'Can you?'

'I have to.'

They stared at each other, aware of the tension rising. Ed wondered if it always would be like this between them. And what made it worse was that each was trying to do the best for the other. Both knew it.

'All right,' Nick said eventually. 'The best thing will be if we go together. I can hand over my surgery. You get ready, meet me down at the harbour in half an hour and I'll find a fisherman to take us out to the ship.'

As he spoke there was the first rattle of rain against the window-panes.

'Get a good one,' said Ed. 'There's a storm brewing.'

'They're all good. Now let's move.'

Ed went first to the surgery dispensary, where he signed himself out a large quantity of antibiotics. He knew there would be antibiotics on board, medical centres on cruise ships were always well equipped, especially with anything needed to deal with gastroenteritis. But he liked to make sure. Then he drove home, packed a small bag with whatever clothes and toiletries he might need for a two or three day stay. Practice again. It wasn't the first time he'd had to pack in a hurry.

Then down to the harbour. The rain had slowed a little but now the winds were starting. Ed looked at the sky, at the sea. This was going to be a really bad one.

His father was at the end of the jetty, waving to him. A fishing boat danced madly up and down below him. As Ed strode down the jetty he wondered how his father was feeling. In 1998 there had been a disaster in Penhally. During a storm like this a sea rescue had ended in tragedy. Among others, Nick's father and brother had both died that night.

So how did Nick feel now? Ed wondered. For that matter, how did he feel himself? His uncle and his grand-father, both remembered, both loved, and both dead.

He reached the end of the jetty, climbed carefully down an iron ladder and jumped aboard the heaving fishing boat. The fisherman grabbed his arm, helped him into the tiny cabin. 'Going to be a bad one,' he said, echoing Ed's own thoughts, 'and it's going to get worse.'

They were taken to the lee of the ship where the boarding platform had been rigged. It was still a hard job, jumping across. But both Ed and Nick were fit, and soon they were being taken up stairs and along companionways to the captain's cabin.

Ed took to the captain at once. He recognised the

military training, the ability to see a problem and try to sort it out, no matter what the cost.

'My first concern is the safety of the passengers,' the Captain told them. 'And their safety comes before their comfort. I will do whatever you think fit. I've been in touch with the port authorities, and the ship in effect is now quarantined.' He looked at Nick. 'Dr Tremayne, they'd like you to send them a report. My head office is not very happy—they're losing money.' He smiled without mirth. 'Well, that's just too bad. Since I spoke to you I've spoken to the passengers and explained the situation. All ill or possibly ill passengers will be confined to their cabins, where food and medical attention will be brought to them. I've ordered a VSP—a vessel sanitation programme—and had as much of the ship as possible disinfected. At my nurse's suggestion I've stopped self-service at meal times.'

'You obviously know what to do in cases like this,' Ed said approvingly.

The captain's smile was bitter. 'We've been to the Indian Ocean. When passengers and crew return from a visit on shore, each one of them is handed a napkin and told to rub their hands with it. It contains a disinfectant that is supposed to kill all known germs and viruses. My crew constantly wipe down and disinfect all handrails in the ship. And I've made sure these precautions have been carried out thoroughly! And then this happens when we're nearly home.'

Ed nodded. 'You seem to have done all you can, Captain.'

'There's more. I don't know if you realise it, but all medical attention has to be paid for. The one exception is stomach upsets. Passengers are told very clearly that if they have any suspicion of a gastric problem they are to phone the medical centre and all medical care will be free.'

Ed was impressed. 'With all these precautions it seems unfair that you should be struck down like this. But you are prepared.'

'An old military rule. Hope for the best, plan for the worst. Now you'll be taken down to the medical section and I leave you to do what you can. Please, let me know at once if there's anything you need.'

'I like a man who knows what he wants,' Nick muttered to him as they were led along companionways.

'You can always tell a military mind,' Ed muttered back. 'But I'm desperately trying to lose mine. I'm a doctor, not a soldier.'

Ed still felt a little uneasy. He knew his father was watching him, looking for any sign of weakness. But he had been in large-scale disease outbreaks before. The fact that he had lost… He forced himself to keep his memories and his feelings in check. But he knew it would be hard.

There was no one in the medical centre when they arrived and the steward left them there to find the nurse. Both took the opportunity to look around. There was a reception area and two treatment rooms, one of which could double up as an operating theatre. It even had X-ray facilities. There was a minilab, a pharmacy and five tiny wards. To one side was a corridor with the staff's living quarters leading off it. It was a hospital and GP surgery combined and in miniature.

Behind him Ed heard a feminine voice say, 'Nick! It's good to see you again.'

'Maddy, it's good to see you, too. You were the best nurse I ever had.'

Ed turned to see his father stooping to kiss the cheek of a petite woman in nurse's uniform. Then Nick stood aside and said, 'Maddy, I'd like you to meet another Dr Tremayne. My son Ed.'

Ed held his hand out. 'Pleased to meet you, Maddy.' And then he looked at her properly. She was about his own age, and had shoulder-length light brown hair, now carefully tied back. Her body was curvaceous. She was very attractive. Then he tried to distance himself from that thought. He was only a doctor here!

Maddy smiled at him, and he found himself looking into her eyes. They were large, hazel-coloured and rather beautiful. But for the moment it was the expression in them that concerned him. There was apprehension there, but that was to be expected in someone who was faced with an outbreak of illness. And something more. Ed had a sense that something was haunting her, a fear perhaps, or a memory.

He thought that he'd like to know more about Maddy, perhaps help her get over whatever it was that was troubling her. He could feel her anguish—after all, he had suffered anguish himself.

But first he had his duty to attend to! 'So how can we help you, Maddy?' he asked.

'I'd like you to tell me I'm wrong. But I know I'm not. I've now got fifteen people confined to their cabins and there are more who're about to go down sick. At the moment I'm the only trained medical staff but there are stewards who've been on an elementary course and they can act as orderlies. They've been very good. The illness is…' She corrected herself. 'I think the illness is caused by Norovirus. Acute gastroenteritis. But it seems to be much more serious than normal.'

'Is that possible in this country?' Ed asked. 'I thought that for Europeans, who are reasonably well fed, it was nasty but not too dangerous.'

There was a pause. Then Nick said, 'I'm afraid there are variations. Some quite recent mutations. And some of them can be very unpleasant indeed.'

'You've dealt with them before?'

'Only in the lab,' Nick said.

Maddy was pleased to have Nick and Ed there. She felt confident that she could have coped with the outbreak alone somehow. But with the Tremaynes helping her work, coping would be easier.

She could tell the two were father and son. It was not just the physical resemblance—though that was there. The were both big, tall, handsome men. More important was the feelings they inspired, their attitude. They seemed calm, competent, tough.

Or was that just the way she remembered Nick? He didn't seem to have changed much since she'd last seen him. His dark hair was perhaps a little more grey, there was the odd extra line on his face. But he was as lean, as erect as ever.

Ed was different. His hair was blond, cut very short. His eyes were blue, unlike his father's brown ones. And he moved differently, lightly, almost on his toes. Maddy recognised it as the action of a well-trained athlete.

They were both very different from the men she had been mixing with recently. Apart from the crew, most of the men were old. Dr Coombs was short, a bit tubby and was never going to die of overwork. She was feeling more confident by the minute.

'So what have you got for us, Maddy?' Nick asked.

She gave a quick summary of what had happened so far. 'The captain is doing what he can, confining the sick ones to their cabins, taking all possible precautions. The passengers here have been well fed, well looked after. But a lot of them are old, or have come on this cruise to convalesce. I've dealt with gastroenteritis before, I know it's not supposed to be too serious. But the vital signs in some of them are very worrying.'

'Might I glance through the case notes?' Nick asked. She had them ready and handed them to him.

He passed half of the pile of notes to Ed and both started to skim through them. After a while Nick muttered, 'This does seem to be more serious than…'

'May I see the rest of the notes?' Ed asked him, and the two exchanged piles. Then there was silence for a moment and Maddy felt her confidence ebbing. It was good to be proved right…but she didn't want to be right.

Ed spoke first. 'I agree with you, Maddy. This is bad. I've come across an attack like this before. People think that gastroenteritis has just one cause but there can be many. In this case, onset seems far too rapid to be normal, dehydration far too advanced. It looks like a particularly effective bacterium or virus.'

'Most likely a virus,' Nick put in.

Ed shrugged. 'We'll have to find out. To be more exact,

you'll have to find out. But my experience says that it is a bacterium. Note the consistent high temperatures. More in line with bacterium than virus.'

'A viral infection is more common.'

'True. But I intend to use antibiotics until you tell me definitely that this is a virus.'

Maddy realised that this was a small trial of strength between the two men. Between father and son—both doctors. There was a difference of opinion and she knew that Nick didn't like being contradicted.

There was a silence and then Nick said slowly, 'We agreed that you are in charge. You must do what you think best.'

Ed nodded. 'I'd like you to do the necessary tests and let me know the results as quickly as possible. Analysis is one of your strengths.' He looked at Maddy. 'How busy were you before this outbreak? You've obviously got more cases than these.'

'I've been kept busy,' she said. 'There's the usual small stuff—minor injuries, conditions that need an eye kept on them. This morning I had a man who'd had a TIA—I think.'

'Would you like me to have a look at him?' Ed asked.

She appreciated being asked. 'I'm reasonably happy but, yes,' she said. 'If you don't mind.'

'I don't mind, I'm a doctor. I'll be happy to.' He smiled at her then—she realised for the first time. And it made his face, the sometimes stern Tremayne face, look so much more attractive.

'One good thing,' he went on, 'is that this condition tends to burn out very quickly. Only a forty-eight hour isolation period is needed. Now, shall we go and check on the patients so far?'

They agreed that Nick should visit the male patients with a steward, and she would visit the female patients with Ed. They set off at once.

As they paced along the corridor she was aware of an odd sensation. At first she didn't recognise it, it just seemed that the world might not be as bad a place as it had seemed a few minutes ago. There was promise in it. Then it struck her, so suddenly that for a moment she stopped walking. It was Ed Tremayne! He was…she was…she was attracted to him! This was ludicrous!

Her felt her stop, turned to her. 'Everything OK?'

'Just something I thought I had forgotten,' she mumbled. 'Nothing important.'

She tried to examine what she was feeling. It was just relief, she decided. There was something solid and dependable about Ed. Whatever attraction there was, it wasn't sexual. Was it? But he was attractive—both physically and in his personality, And there was something hidden about him—she couldn't work out quite what it was…

'Which branch of the armed forces were you in, Ed?' she asked, hoping her voice sounded normal.

He laughed. 'How did you know that I'd been in the armed forces?'

That was an easy question to answer. 'Well, there's the short haircut. But more than that, I've had dealings with soldiers before. There's something about the way they behave that I recognise. It's the way they look round, assessing everything. Then the certainty that they are right. Often the way they are ready to take charge.'

A small smile. 'So you expect me to take charge? Maddy, I've no intention of doing that. I've said it and I meant it—we're partners. And I've always thought of myself as a doctor far more than a soldier. As to being certain that I'm right, well, no. I've been wrong, very wrong. And later I've realised it.'

His voice went quiet as he spoke, as if an unwelcome memory had flashed across his mind. For a moment she wondered what he was thinking, but she decided it wasn't the right time to ask. 'We all make mistakes,' she said. 'It's part of the human condition.'

'True.' His voice was mild as he went on, 'but I do have to own up. I am an ex-soldier and some of the happiest days of my life were when I was in the army.' He paused a moment and then said, 'But not necessarily because I was in the army.'

'Right,' she said.

CHAPTER THREE

ED HAD skimmed through her notes and decided that this was the patient he wanted to see first. She had been one of the earliest to fall ill, and her condition appeared to be one of the worst.

Miriam Jones was a widow of sixty-eight. She was not happy with her condition. 'I paid a lot of money for this trip, Dr Tremayne,' she said after Ed had introduced himself. 'I do not take kindly to having to spend the last two days of it lying on a bed in my cabin.'

But her voice was weak. Maddy could see that a lot of the strength had gone out of someone who had previously been a tough lady. She was trying to survive—but she was failing.

Ed examined her. Maddy had already set up a giving set to get fluids into the patient but Ed suggested a more rapid rate of flow. He also prescribed a larger dose of the antibiotic that Maddy had already given her. Then he took Mrs Jones's hand.

'I'm not going to hide anything from you, Mrs Jones,' he said. 'You're seriously ill. But I've got confidence in you, I know you've got the strength to pull through. And I know you won't be as much trouble as some others we're seeing.'

Mrs Jones's pale face lit up. 'No, I won't,' she said.

'Then I'll be in to see you later. Anything really serious, phone us.'

The next call was totally different. Miss Owen—the new Miss Owen, having previously been Mrs Dacre and now very satisfactorily divorced—had come on this cruise to 'rebuild her confidence'. Contracting gastroenteritis had shaken this confidence.

Maddy saw Ed handle this patient in a totally different fashion. He joked with her. Even got a smile. And when they left the cabin, Miss Owen was a slightly happier person.

They worked their way through the rest of the cases. Most cabins were occupied by couples. Maddy noticed that when this was the case, Ed was as charming as ever with the sick person. But then he took the husband or wife to one side and had a quiet word with them. She managed to listen to one conversation and was intrigued by it. Ed's words were partly reassurance and partly a clear statement of what he expected. Ed knew what the patients needed and was going to see that they got it.

Finally they had seen all the cases and were walking back to the medical centre to meet Nick again. Maddy felt that this was going to be a good partnership. 'I'm glad you've come on board,' she said. 'I feel that things aren't too bad now.'

He glanced at her, smiled. 'So, for the moment, have you got over your bitterness at the military mind? Tell me, was it the army as a whole or one particular individual?'

This took her aback. Ed was an astute observer, far more perceptive than she had realised. 'Sorry if I was a bit short with you,' she muttered. 'I'm sure we'll work well together.'

She wasn't going to answer his question about her being upset by one particular individual. She waited for him to ask again but he didn't. He knew she didn't want to answer and that made her even more cautious.

She didn't want to reveal herself, to be vulnerable. And Ed was getting close to making her feel exposed.

They turned a corner and saw a mother and child coming towards them. The little boy, aged about seven, ran towards her, yelling, 'Nurse Maddy! Look, I'm a pirate again.'

And a pirate little Robbie Cowley was. He flourished a large plastic cutlass, had a skull and crossbones on his large plastic hat. His T-shirt didn't quite match, though. On it was the picture of a devil, cheerful rather than frightening. There was a dressing on his right arm.

Laughing, Maddy was about to pick him up then remembered where she had just been. The less contact between people the better.

'Just stay there, Robbie,' she said with a smile to reassure him. 'There might be some nasty stuff on me.' Then she turned to the mother and smiled. 'Don't tell me, Mrs Cowley, he's still a handful.'

Mrs Cowley, a buxom blonde in her early thirties, smiled and shook her head. 'I thought when he cut his arm that it would quieten him down a bit. You told him he had to be good, not to run around so much or he might hurt his arm even more. And he was good, didn't run around. For about twenty minutes.'

'That's little boys for you,' Maddy agreed. 'You just have to be there with them all the time.' She turned and said to Ed, 'This is Mrs Cowley and her son Robbie. I've seen quite a bit of young Robbie.' She twinkled at the little boy. 'He's been a regular customer—that devil on his T-shirt says it all.'

'I'm a pirate now, not a devil,' Robbie shouted. 'What nasty stuff on you? I'll hit it with my cutlass.'

Ed stopped a cutlass swing with his arm, and crouched down to face Robbie. 'That's a fine weapon you have there, Captain,' he said, 'and a fine hat, too. What's the name of your ship?'

'The Hisp…the Hisp thingy,' Robbie said. 'After Nurse Maddy had bandaged up my arm she read me a bit about it. It was good!'

'She's a good reader. I'll get her to read to me. Now, you will be careful with that deadly weapon, won't you?'

Maddy watched curiously. Ed had work to do but from his body language it was obvious that he was clearly taken with the little boy. There was regret in the way he straightened himself, became a doctor again.

'I'm going to capture a ship,' Robbie told him. 'One of those white ones on the top deck.'

'I wish you luck. A pirate's life is a hard one.'

There was time for a few polite words with Mrs Cowley and then they moved back to the medical centre. 'You seemed to quite take to Robbie,' Maddy suggested.

'Typical little boy. I like them.' A clipped reply. 'Is his father on board?'

'There is no father. And Mrs Cowley has just been diagnosed with adult-onset diabetes. She has the pills, she knows—or she should know—how to control her diet. But she relapses. I've kept an eye on her, tried to get her to discipline herself. But if you like eating then a cruise ship is the last thing you want to be on.'

'So Mrs Cowley has spent quite some time resting in her cabin? And Robbie has been allowed to run riot?'

'There are two big children's playgrounds and staff always on duty. But no way can they keep track of every child. Robbie was trying to climb onto a lifeboat but he fell and gashed his arm. Before that he tumbled down some stairs and trapped his fingers in a door.'

'But a cheerful child?'

'He's lovely,' Maddy agreed.

There was a message from the captain waiting for them when they got back to the medical centre. The storm had got worse and the forecast was that over the next twelve hours it would get worse still. It would be extremely difficult, probably impossible, to try to move ill people from the ship to land. A helicopter landing was out of the question, a boat trip would be highly dangerous.

'I don't think we want to start moving old sick people anyway,' Nick said, 'but we'll have to decide if it's necessary. What do you think, Maddy, Ed?'

Maddy was pleased that she was included in the decision-making. But she decided to remain silent for a while. Perhaps she was too close to the problem.

'It's gastroenteritis all right,' Ed said, 'but it's a very nasty strain. I still suspect it's bacterial in origin.'

Nick shook his head. 'We can't be certain until I've done tests,' he said. 'I've collected samples, and we'll know more when I've been inside the lab for a while.'

He looked at his son, a glance half compassionate, half assessing, Maddy thought. There was something here that she didn't know about. And she wanted to know what.

'We're agreed that Maddy needs help—that one of us should stay aboard?'

'We're agreed. There's just too much work for one person. And I'm the obvious one to stay.'

'Are you sure you'll be all right?' Nick asked.

'I'll be fine.'

Another silence. Maddy wondered what was happening. There seemed to be some silent exchange of messages between the two men. She could read it in their body language. Nick was relaxed, trying to be helpful. Ed had the taut look of a man who was expecting an argument. Finally Nick said, 'Right, then. Still, remember, a good doctor will ask for help if he needs it. Now I'm going to see the captain, explain the situation and tell him what we think it's best to do. Then the final decision will be his. But unless he objects, Ed, you stay, do what you can, and remember that the next twelve to twenty-four hours will be the hardest.'

'I've dealt with that before,' Ed said.

'Good. Oh, the patients I've just seen, there's one, a Mr Simmonds. He's got gastroenteritis all right and I've given him a thorough examination—he's an old man but there's nothing seriously wrong with him. Nothing physical, that is.'

'But mentally?' Ed asked.

'Well, I noticed he's on antidepressants—mild ones. When I asked him about them he said they did little good, he'd stopped taking them and he felt better. But…I've got a feeling about the man.'

Ed shook his head. 'I'll keep an eye on him,' he said, 'but I suspect there'll be nothing we can do. We just have to hope.'

'Sometimes that's all a doctor can do,' his father said. Then he turned to Maddy. 'Been good to see you, Maddy. Hope you and Ed get on well together. I've every confidence in the pair of you.' And then he was gone.

Maddy and Ed looked at each other. 'This morning we didn't even know the other one existed,' Maddy said hesitantly, 'and now we're thrown together like this.'

'Strange, how things happen. But I'm looking forward to working with you. Getting to know you better.'

That was a statement that could be taken more than one way, Maddy thought. But as they looked at each other he didn't say anything more. There seemed to be some kind of understanding flowing between them that, just for the moment, didn't need words. His blue eyes stared at her. She could see puzzlement there, as if he didn't really know what he was feeling. But finally he jerked them back into the present.

'Let's get started,' he said. 'Now, are there any scrubs I could borrow?'

She pointed to a cupboard. 'One thing about being on a cruise ship, the laundry is done fast and well.'

'It's going to need to be that way,' Ed said. 'During a gastroenteritis outbreak, cleanliness is all important. Now we need to see what resources we—'

The phone rang. Maddy picked up the receiver, listened for a moment. 'Cabin B52? We'll be right there.' She looked at Ed. 'Another case. It's going to be like this non-stop now, isn't it?'

'It is. And there's your regular work, too.' He smiled again. 'But we'll manage together.'

He decided to change into scrubs before they set off.

When he came back in the green shapeless garments she noticed the muscles on his forearms. And she noticed something else. He was wearing a wedding ring.

For some reason she was disappointed, which was silly. She should have known. A good-looking man like Ed would obviously be married. He would have been snapped up years ago. What was she thinking of? Anyway, she was off men. It was foolish on her part, harbouring even the smallest feeling for him. They were just colleagues for a while.

They went to Cabin B52 and examined the patient—a man this time. There was the usual initial assessment. A high temperature suggested bacterial infection rather than viral. Hypotension—low blood pressure—was another indicator. There would be tachycardia—a fast pulse, and often it would be thready. The most obvious signs were of dehydration. A dry mouth, no tears, skin that tented when it was pinched, poor capillary return, tested by pinching the fingernails. There would be mild discomfort to the abdomen—but it didn't get worse when palpated. Either she or Ed would take a blood sample and test it in the medical centre.

And there was always the chance that it could be some other condition. It would be foolish to assume that any illness was automatically gastroenteritis.

To avoid dehydration each patient had to be given a saline and dextrose IV line. The amount given depended on physical state, body weight and the blood count. Since Ed had decided that this was a bacterial infection, not a viral one, antibiotics could be used. But the kind and the amount and the frequency depended on the patient's state.

And the seriousness of the attack. Some people were more susceptible than others.

As before, after this assessment Ed spoke to the man's partner and told her what to expect, what to do. Again, as before, Maddy was impressed by the clear way he spoke, by the manner in which he made it clear that he expected his suggestions to be carried out. The passengers certainly seemed calmed by him.

But Maddy still felt a little unsettled. Working with Ed was not as satisfying as it had been before.

As they walked back to the medical centre she asked, as casually as she could, 'Ed, will your wife mind you being away for a while?'

'Why do you think I have a wife?' The question was abrupt, hostile even.

'Well, it's just that I saw you were wearing a wedding ring. I'm sorry if I upset you.'

'You didn't upset me.' But his tone contradicted his words. 'My wife is dead.'

She wondered if he was going to say any more, then wondered if she ought to say she was sorry again. But he said nothing, pacing more quickly down the corridor so she had to hurry to keep up with him.

Obviously she had upset him. She wondered if all relationships had to result in pain.

When they got back to the medical centre Ed became his normal efficient self again. 'We know the situation is going to deteriorate,' he said, 'and we need to get on top of it now. I'd like to check on all supplies. If necessary, we might have to get in some more. Somehow.'

'I'll write out an inventory of the most needed drugs,' Maddy said, 'we can mark them off as we use them, so we know when we're getting low.'

'Good idea. And shall we have a list of the stewards we can call on and work out a rota? If you want to pencil in any personal comments, I'll see them but they'll go no further.'

'You've done this kind of thing before, haven't you?' she asked.

'I have.'

She noticed he didn't give her any details. For a moment there was a hunted look on his face, as if there was a painful memory. But when he spoke he was as clear and forceful as ever. 'What's very useful is to have a wall chart, marking off each patient we have, the stage of development of the illness, the treatment. It's important that we can see at a glance just what the situation is. A set of patient's notes that you have to page through just isn't good enough.' He thought for a moment. 'In fact, could we have a steward or someone in here to act as ward secretary?'

'I'll phone the captain, see if he can find someone for us. I'm sure he will.'

'Good. Is there anything special that you—?'

The phone rang again. This tine it was Ed who answered it, who took the number of the cabin and then said, 'I'll be right there.'

He looked at Maddy. 'Looks like another case. I'll take this one on my own—you've got plenty to do here organising the logistics of this operation. I'll be back to liaise as soon as I can.'

Back to liaise? Maddy thought as soon as he had gone. Had she joined the army without knowing it? Then she realised. Everything Ed had done made perfect sense. This was an emergency and he was treating it as such. He was concerned about the welfare of his patients. Then she remembered something else. There had been a set expression on his face as he'd talked about the organisation necessary. As if this was—or had been—painful. What was he hiding?

She had finished the paperwork when he returned and told him that the captain was sending them down a purser's assistant to act as ward clerk. He nodded approvingly. 'I hate paperwork,' he said, 'but I know it's vital to keep it up. Now we can concentrate on the important work. Maddy, did you tell me that you thought that one of your patients had a TIA this morning?'

She nodded. 'Mr Bryce. I got a steward to keep an eye on him, but I'd like to go and see him myself.'

'Let's go together. Are the case notes handy?'

He scanned the notes and she saw him frown. 'If we were on shore, I'd send this man to hospital,' he said.

'So would I. But this morning I thought that shipping him ashore might be more of a risk than keeping him in his bed. That was when I thought that we'd dock tomorrow. And now, with the disease and the storm, it's impossible.'

'You still made the right decision. Let's go and look at him.'

So they went. And it was obvious that Mr Bryce was a very sick man indeed. Now his speech was slurred, he was much weaker. Maddy watched helplessly as Ed listened to Mr Bryce's heart, took his blood pressure, talked gently to him.

'You've enjoyed the cruise, then, Mr Bryce? Thinking of coming back on another one?'

'If I'm alive, yes.' Maddy saw a tiny smile on her friend's face. 'And if Maddy there is on the ship.'

'Maddy is a star. I've only just met her but I can tell that.'

'That's a nice thing to say. Yes, Maddy is a star.' Mr Bryce's eyes closed.

Ed changed Maddy's prescription of aspirin for warfarin—a much more effective anti-coagulant. Then he shook Mr Bryce's hand and told him that they'd be back to see him.

'How is he?' Maddy asked, knowing and dreading what the answer would be.

'He's an old man and I think there's a danger of a stroke,' Ed said. 'But, Maddy, no one can tell. He has a fighting chance and he looks like a fighter. Was he a particular friend of yours?'

'Sort of,' Maddy said. 'I've seen a lot of him. Ed, you were kind to him.'

'I try to be kind to all my patients,' he said. 'When it's possible.'

After that cases came in with predictable regularity. Ed saw each one first, made an initial diagnosis—which was usually not difficult. More difficult was assessing the seriousness of the attack and deciding on the medication. This was a task Maddy was pleased to hand over. After Ed's initial visit, Maddy took over the nursing duties.

Here again, things weren't as normal. Ed had to warn her. 'Maddy, this is an emergency, you can't give each patient the time you would in a normal nursing situation. You're a specialist and you must learn to delegate. Whatever a steward can do, get him or her to do it. You're needed for the special nursing jobs.'

She didn't like what she had to do, leaving patients who needed and wanted her skills. Needed her care. But she knew that Ed's apparent ruthlessness made sense.

As the day wore on the situation got worse. More and more people were falling ill. The captain came down to see them. He said, 'I'm not going to stay, not going to interfere. Whatever you need, just ask for it. If it's available, you can have it.' And he was gone.

'Good man, the captain,' was Ed's remark.

They were coping—just. But they knew that they'd have to be up all night. 'Don't worry,' Ed told her, 'whatever happens, we'll manage. We'll manage because we're a team, we're working together.'

She liked him for this. She wasn't exactly enjoying herself—but Ed made her feel as if her work was worthwhile, he gave her a sense of purpose. She liked working with him.

They worked together until the evening. Maddy was sitting in the medical centre, checking over the supplies. Ed had gone what he called wandering. 'Just ambling about, dropping in here and there,' he said. 'Getting the feel of things.'

Then after fifteen minutes, she was buzzed. 'Hi, Maddy, Ed here.' It had only been ten minutes since she had seen him. But she was surprised at how welcome his voice was. What was happening to her? Then she recognised the tone of his voice, quiet, regretful. This wasn't good news.

'Who is it, Ed?'

'It's Mr Bryce. He's…very ill but he's asking for you.'

'Mr Bryce?' An old man but the one true friend she had made on the voyage. 'How is he, Ed?'

There was a hesitation, then the usual careful doctor-speak. 'He's very ill, very weak. There's nothing more we can do for him. But he's lucid—now.'

Maddy got the message. Her friend Malcolm Bryce was dying. She had managed to visit him twice that day, though if she had not been so busy she would have stayed with him much longer. But she just hadn't had time! And now he was dying. Maddy bit her lip, trying to stop the tears squeezing from beneath her lids. Why did it have to happen to her friend?

'All right if I come to see him?'

Ed understood what she was asking. 'Of course. If you'd like to stay with him a while, I have other things to do.'

'I'm on my way.'

She only needed one glance at Malcolm to know that he didn't have very long. To a trained nurse the signs were obvious. But he was still awake, he recognised her and smiled when she took his hand.

'Something to say to you, Maddy,' he managed to whisper. 'I don't think I'll have the chance again. When I asked you to marry me—I know it was a joke, but I half meant it.'

She smiled sadly at the old man. 'I told you, Malcolm,

just now I don't want to get married. But if I did, you'd be the man I'd pick.'

'I don't think I can wait. But if I'd been forty years younger then I would have waited. But, Maddy, you'll make some other man very happy.'

'Perhaps,' she replied, and squeezed his hand. Then she watched as his eyes closed and he lapsed into unconsciousness. She knew he wouldn't open them again.

She was tired, she needed to go to bed. But Malcolm had been her friend, she did not want him to die alone. So she sat in a chair and listened to his laboured breathing. The nicest man she had met in a long time—and he was going to die. She couldn't help it. Silently, the tears came.

It didn't come as a shock when there was a quiet tap on the door, and Ed came in. He said nothing, glanced at Mr Bryce then raised his eyebrows at her. She shook her head. Nothing could be done. But he was still a doctor, he made a quick but gentle examination—and apparently agreed with her.

'I'm going to stay with him for a while longer,' she said.

'Well, I'm entitled to a bit of self-indulgence. I'll stay, too.' He sat by her, looked at her as she sat there with her head bowed. 'Was he a particular friend?'

'Perhaps he was. He had to come to the medical centre quite a bit, he'd hurt his leg—and this morning he asked me to marry him.'

'He what?'

Maddy managed to smile. 'It was only a joke. Or perhaps half a joke. But I liked him a lot.'

Both of then looked up as the sound of Mr Bryce's breathing altered. Cheyne-Stokes breathing. An alteration from very rapid to very slow breaths, with pauses between them. In a man of Mr Bryce's condition it meant that death was near.

'He was the first man to be nice to me for quite a long time,' she said.

Ed looked surprised. 'The first man to be nice to you? I would have thought that there was no shortage of men interested in you. You're very attractive, Maddy, you must know that.'

She felt a small pleasure at hearing him say this, but at the moment she had other things on her mind. 'Perhaps so. You know this morning—was it only this morning, it seems so long ago? I got a phone call. It was from my ex-boyfriend, ex-fiancé if you like. For a while I thought I was going to marry him. I wanted to have babies with him. Anyway, he wants to pick up with me again. And I don't want to… I just can't… Though I do feel guilty.'

'Why should you feel guilty? Better to decide early that you're not suited.'

'I'm a nurse, I'm supposed to heal the sick. And he was sick.'

She wasn't surprised when Ed took her hand. 'Why don't you tell me about it? I'll try to help if I can. Or help you to understand.'

She laughed, without humour. 'That might be possible. The two of you have things in common.'

He raised his eyebrows again, but all he said was, 'I'd like to help.'

She sighed. 'We got engaged. It was a lightning court-ship, he was a hard man to resist. He was a soldier, he went off on active service and he came home with PTSD—

post-traumatic stress disorder. And after that things got so bad that I had to get away from him. It was classic mental abuse—but I suspected that if I married him the mental abuse would have turned physical in time. I was…scared. In fact, at times I still am.'

'Did he have any treatment?'

'He went to a clinic a couple of times at first. Then he said it was a waste of time and that he was cured. He wouldn't take the medication he was prescribed.'

'Tell me more about him. What had he in common with me?'

'He was decisive like you. He knew what he wanted, was going to get it because he thought he was right. It's good if you want to get something done. It's not so good if you're the one being done to. He just can't or won't accept that we're finished. And we are!'

'Have you a family to offer you support? Are your parents alive?'

'I've got no one. My parents died a while ago now, before this happened, and they had no relations. You said I was attractive, well, apparently I am. And because of that, I found that too often men were out for just what they could get. I had a couple of rotten experiences. Then I met Brian. And at first he was different. At first.'

'I see,' he said. Then, with a small smile, 'Maddy, you might not like it but I'm going to be decisive. Obviously your ex-fiancé needs treatment. I'm a doctor, I've had experience of army cases. I can make some phone calls, see that he's picked up and given proper attention. He obviously didn't get it before. But some of the army psychiatrists are very good indeed. They can help.'

There was something odd in his tone, at first she couldn't work out what. But then she realised. It was pain, the pain of memory. She lifted her head to look at him and said, 'You say that as if you know it from personal experience.'

There was a hesitation before he said, 'I was sent for psychological assessment. I had to have a couple of consultations, whether I wanted them or not.'

'Sent because you were showing signs of some kind of mental problem?'

He laughed, but there was no humour in his laughter. 'Just the opposite. It was thought that…that I had suffered things that ought to produce mental problems, but I showed no signs of them.'

'What kind of things that ought to produce mental problems?'

His reply was definitive. 'I don't talk about them.'

But she still wanted to know more. 'So why didn't you show signs of them?'

'I could say because I was tough,' he said. 'But I know that I was just lucky.'

She thought she could believe that. 'And you were given a clean bill of health? No psychological problems found, no irrational fears or phobias?'

'None.'

Just one simple, curt word. But for some reason it didn't convince her. 'Are you sure?'

He lifted his arms, in a gesture almost of surrender. 'Psychology isn't like medicine. It isn't true or false, right or wrong, good or bad. There are great grey areas. And if a psychologist digs hard enough, he's bound to find something not quite right.'

'Are you going to tell me what they found that was not quite right about you?'

'No,' he said.

'Are you going to tell me what things you suffered that caused these problems?'

'No.'

Apparently he thought that the conversation had run its course. But there were more things Maddy wanted to know. She thought that she was getting close to the real Ed, and she wanted desperately to hear more. She started…

It wasn't a sound, it was a lack of sound. Both were trained, both knew what had happened. They turned to look at their patient. Mr Bryce had stopped breathing altogether.

Neither Maddy nor Ed spoke or moved for a while. Then Maddy moved over to look at her friend, bent to kiss him on the forehead.

'You're tired,' Ed said. 'And there's nothing more you can do. I'll do the paperwork and see to everything, it's better if you don't do it. He was your friend, his last few minutes were made happier because you were here. Just go back to the centre, try to close your eyes, relax a little.'

She looked at him through tear-shrouded eyes. 'You're a kind man, Ed.'

'I'm just doing my job,' he said gruffly.

It was eleven o'clock at night, and they were lucky—there was a slight lull in things. She made herself a mug of tea and sat and thought about Ed. He was like her. There was some burden he was carrying—and she wanted to know what it was. She'd only known him a few hours, but during that time she'd seen enough of him to know he was a caring and sensitive man. She could even come to… No, she couldn't. The fear was still deep inside her.

He walked into the medical centre a few minutes later and smiled at her, a weary smile. 'We're getting there,' he said.

'We're getting there because we're working together.' She stood, walked up to him, touched his arm. Just a gentle indication of her liking. 'I couldn't have managed without you.'

'I suspect,' he said, 'that you could.'

Afterwards she wondered, didn't exactly know how it had happened. They were both tired, of course, perhaps not entirely certain of what they were doing. Perhaps it was a purely spontaneous act, something that happened without either of them knowing why.

He looked down at her hand on his arm. Very slowly, he slid his other arm round her waist. It was warm, comforting, she leaned back against it.

His eyes were very blue. She could see them clearly, they were looking down at her with a half curious, half intent expression. Beautiful blue eyes. Why hadn't she noticed how beautiful they were before?

His lips touched hers. So tentatively she knew that she could break away in a second. But she didn't want to. In fact, she reached up, slipped her arm around his neck. At first a gentle kiss. Then it deepened. It turned into something much more than she had anticipated. His body pressed closer to hers. But she was only half-aware of it, all she could think of was the kiss and how it made her head spin, and how Ed was like no man she'd ever met and—

The phone rang and they sprang apart.

Ed picked up the phone, no sign of emotion in his face as he listened intently. 'You're sure? Yes, that sounds right. OK, I'll be there in five minutes.'

'Work calls,' he said to Maddy. Then he shook his head, looked puzzled. 'I'm sorry that happened,' he said. 'It was my fault. I shouldn't have kissed you. We're working hard, we're stressed, we daren't get involved with each other. Emotion and this kind of situation… I've been here before and it's…it's bad.'

Things were different now, but Maddy was still trying to make sense of what had happened. Above all, make sense of how much she had enjoyed it.

'You might be right,' she said, 'and I don't know why we did that. It must be because we are both tired. I don't usually kiss—I mean, kiss like that—people who I've only just met.'

'And I don't go around kissing people like that either,' he said. 'But this is a time apart. And it's a world apart— being on a cruise ship is fundamentally unreal. We've both got lives to go back to. Then we'll forget this.'

'Of course we'll forget it,' she agreed. But as she looked at him, she wondered if either of them believed her. The kiss had been so wonderful.

There was one thing she had to add. 'But, Ed, whatever it was, it wasn't bad.'

CHAPTER FOUR

IT WAS at half past eleven that they were called in to Mrs Jones's room. She had fought valiantly, but now her body was weary. The steward observing had called Ed, and Ed took Maddy with him.

Ed thanked the steward, then nodded for her to go. Then he examined Mrs Jones and then said to Maddy, 'She still has a chance. A small one. All we can do is wait.'

They sat together in silence. Then she thought that this was the man who not fifteen minutes ago had kissed her. And had apparently enjoyed it. Where had he gone now?

He moved over to Mrs Jones, leaned over her and checked her condition. 'Perhaps a bit of an improvement,' he muttered, 'but we'll see.'

Maddy realised that he was calming himself by acting as a doctor. But there were things she wanted to know, he couldn't just leave her with half a story.

'So is all this extra-hard for you?' she asked. 'Does it bring back memories?'

'No. It's not extra-hard. But it is hard. The memories I can deal with, I have to deal with. Now I've got a job to do, I'll do it.' He walked over to their patient, studied her for a minute. 'Maddy, it looks as if Mrs Jones might have rallied a little. I'm going to check on a couple of our other patients, you stay here a while.' He was gone before she could object.

So her chance of questioning him, of learning more about him, had disappeared. She suspected he had left so he didn't have to answer any more of her apparently innocent queries. But when he'd left she found herself wondering. This sudden interest in a man had never happened before.

She had met him for the first time only about twelve hours ago. And twenty minutes ago she had kissed him. Or he had kissed her. Whatever, she knew she had enjoyed it. And this was just not the way she normally behaved. With the departed Dr Coombs and the other nurse she had got on well enough. She'd been popular among both passengers and crew, and she'd enjoyed the dancing in the evening. But she'd only really made friends with Malcolm Bryce, who had been no threat to her heart. And being aboard ship made it easier for her to be pleasant to people and yet be safe. She was never any distance from help, the ship protected her.

So why was Dr Edward Tremayne different?

She felt uneasy. No way was she going to become closely involved with a man again. Not even a man like Ed Tremayne. He seemed to be…different.

She checked Mrs Jones who's condition appeared to be stabilising.

While she was thinking about this, Ed came back. He looked at Mrs Jones and nodded.

She smiled. 'Ed, she's going to be OK. You're doing a really good job.'

She thought at first that he wasn't going to answer, he took so long to reply. But then he said, 'Thanks for being there Maddy. I'm sorry if I'm… It's just this is bringing back so many memories.'

'Even doctors are entitled to feelings,' she told him gently. 'Don't be ashamed of them.'

There was another pause and then he said, 'I just wanted Mrs Jones to have that chance. But I'm sorry if I was a bit short with you.'

Maddy paused for a moment and then said, 'So you're obviously used to emergencies like this. Where were they?'

'Africa.' A curt, one-word answer. But after a moment he said, 'I was an army doctor, went out there expecting to deal with trauma, war wounds, the diseases that a fit soldiery might catch. And I finished up spending most of my time with a starving native population.' He looked at her. 'Come on, there's more patients to see.'

They worked together through the night. Steady but exhausting work. But they knew they were doing a good job.

Maddy was glad she had Ed with her. He seemed to know almost instinctively what was the right dose, the right treatment. She knew she would have done what she could. But Ed was able to do it better. 'You're saving lives,' she told him.

'I've learned how. I've watched other people lose them,' was the flat reply.

She wondered what he was really thinking.

At two in the morning there seemed to be another lull. They both knew it wouldn't last—but it was there. Maddy pointed to her watch. 'This is going to be a long haul,' she said, 'we both know that. You've sent half the stewards off to have some sleep, now you need some yourself. Go to bed, just for a couple of hours. You'll be a better doctor when you wake up.'

'I'd rather you took a break first.'

She shook her head. 'You're showing signs of fatigue now. What time did you get up this morning?'

'I'm an early riser, I was in the sea at six this morning. But I don't need much sleep.'

'I was up a lot later than that and now you need it more than me. Just look at yourself in the mirror.'

She saw him do so, knew he couldn't miss the darkness around his eyes. 'Don't act the macho male with me,' she urged. 'You've got more sense than that. Exhausted doctors make mistakes. Just a couple of hours will improve you no end.'

She could see that he was reluctant to agree but that he had to accept her argument. 'All right, then. But only two hours!'

'After two hours I'll wake you up,' she promised.

She took him to her cabin, pointed to her bed. 'Sleep there. It's my cabin but there's no time to find you somewhere of your own to sleep. And there's a bathroom there if you want it.'

The phone rang. She left him, went to answer it.

He was tired, he had to admit it. And the temptation was just to take off his shoes, lie on the bed and go to sleep.

But he decided not to. He'd have a shower first. Just five minutes would make no end of difference.

He had to smile when he walked into her tiny bathroom. Maddy had not been expecting visitors. On a couple of strings stretched across the shower there were three sets of underwear drying. So far he'd seen her as a nurse, in a rather severe uniform or scrubs. And it suited her. But the knowledge that underneath she wore the flimsiest of coloured lace rather intrigued him.

He had a swift shower, cleaned his teeth. He had brought toiletries with him, in anticipation of his stay on board.

He was still tired but felt considerably better when he climbed into her bed. He decided that he could allow himself another five minutes—but no longer—to think about what he was doing here.

So far he was surviving. He knew he was being efficient, organising the treatments, doing the best possible for his patients. He thought—he hoped—that people felt confident in him.

No one suspected the memories, the terror that swirled underneath. And as he got more fatigued he knew it would get worse, But he would do it. He had to. Only his father would guess what he was going through.

Or had Maddy guessed, too? He had noticed once or twice the thoughtful way that she had looked at him. Her seemingly casual questions had been probing, too. Maddy was quite a woman.

So far he had been thinking about her solely as a colleague. Or had tried to. Now he could think about her as a person. She was so attractive! He was becoming increasingly aware of the generous curves of her body, for some reason emphasised by the plainness of the uniform covering it. When they touched—accidentally, of course— there was that slight electric shock. And the sheen of her hair and the way that it brushed against her cheek when she leaned forward. And he had kissed her! What had possessed him? It was the fact that he was enjoying just being with her and he wanted to— Stop it!

To his horror he realised that he could fall for her. It wasn't just that she was beautiful—though he was coming to appreciate that she was. Ellie Clinton was just as beautiful. Well, nearly as beautiful. And Ellie had nothing like the effect on him that Maddy had. Maddy had some power—a combination of her voice, her figure, her actions, her face… Her face. He remembered that look deep in her eyes… She had been hurt. Like him.

Then he remembered when he had been in a situation like this before. Working in a closed environment with someone he loved. It wasn't good! The risk of tragedy was too great.

Perhaps it would be better if they left each other alone. If they could.

She had intended to leave him for two hours, but after an hour she had to go into her room to wake him. Now she herself was really tired—but she felt that alertness that sometimes came with extreme fatigue.

She switched on the light. She saw his clothes neatly piled, saw him in her bed. The sheet had ridden down, there was a naked shoulder, part of his bare chest. He was muscular—well, she had known that. And was that the end of a scar? Not a medical scar, though.

For a moment she was captivated by the sight of him. He was asleep in her bed, not exactly in her power but something like that. She could look at him, dream, not worry that her feelings might be showing on her face. He was asleep. Then she told herself not to be ridiculous, this was only fatigue. She was not interested in men.

He rolled over onto his back, the blue eyes opened. Briefly she had a glimpse of what he must have looked like as a child as he hovered for a brief moment between being asleep and awake. Innocent, unscarred by life. He would have been a beautiful baby. But he wasn't beautiful now, not exactly. Life had scored lines on his face, made it harsher. And more interesting.

He blinked and intelligence returned to his eyes at once. He was looking at her, recognising her, assessing the situation. However, he was still not fully awake, still not quite his usual guarded self. She thought she saw his pleasure at seeing her. For a moment they just looked at each other, and perhaps some non-verbal message passed. But both seemed to agree that this was not the time to talk about it. Or even to consider it.

'Sorry to wake you early,' she said, 'but we've got an emergency, something quite different.'

'OK, I'm rested.' He sat up, swung a bare leg out of bed and grinned. 'If you wouldn't mind turning your back just for a moment?'

'Oh, yes, of course.' He was naked in her bed! Why did the thought give her a sudden tiny thrill?

There was the rustle of clothes and then he said, 'What's the emergency, then?'

Just the sound of his voice gave her some confidence

but… 'It's the last thing you'd expect, the last thing we need. We're supposed to be coping with an outbreak of gastroenteritis here! Isn't that enough?' The thought of even more work was shocking her.

'Old saying, quoted to us by the captain. "Hope for the best, expect the worst." What's happened?'

'A woman has just gone into labour, I think. She claims the baby's about four weeks premature.'

This did shock him. 'What the hell is a heavily pregnant woman doing on a cruise?'

'Tell me then we'll both know. It's the first I've heard of it. She must have deliberately kept quiet about it. Worn those long floaty dresses. The cruise firm doesn't allow passengers on board who will be over twenty-eight weeks pregnant during the holiday, and for good reason.'

'Right. But she decided she knew best and now we're faced with the problem.' He frowned and Maddy was surprised.

'Childbirth isn't an illness, Ed,' she said gently. 'It's a perfectly normal healthy process.'

She saw him take control of himself. 'Of course. Now we've got her, we'll have to cope. Just how up to date are you with childbirth, Maddy?'

'I'm no midwife. I've watched a few births, been on take a couple of times. If it's straightforward, I could manage. But mostly I've worked in places with a midwifery section. How about you?'

'I did a bit when I was a medical student but nothing much since then. When I was in Africa the people had their own midwives so I was rarely requested for help.'

'That makes sense. Now, I've already phoned the

captain. It's protocol, he has to be informed of events like this. He says he hopes we can cope. The storm has got really bad—nearly hurricane-force winds. If he has to ask for a boat to come out, he will. But he doesn't advise it.'

'No way can we put a pregnant woman into a boat in this weather. It's up to the home team, Maddy.'

She smiled. 'Right. And we've got to be extra-careful not to get the poor little blighter infected. We're still dealing with a gastroenteritis outbreak.'

'I remember,' he said. 'Let's go and see what we can do.'

Maddy was surprised at the bleakness in his voice. True, Ed had worked a full day, and had then had only an hour's sleep. But when she had woken him up he had seemed fine. Only when she'd told him that this was an emergency birth had he seemed upset. She wondered why.

Mr and Mrs Flynn were having their first baby. They had calculated exactly when it was due to be born, worked out that they could have that long-awaited holiday before it was born. There was a month to go. They knew that if they'd told the cruise company that Mrs Flynn was pregnant, they'd never be able to book the cruise. So they hadn't told anyone.

'We never expected this,' Mr Flynn wailed as Maddy and Ed walked into their cabin. 'We thought everything would be all right. I think that it's the storm that's brought it on. All that shaking.'

'Very possibly,' Ed said. 'Now Mr Flynn, if you'd just sit over there and stay calm, we will examine your wife.' He went to Mrs Flynn's side and spoke to her quietly and reassuringly. 'Have your waters broken, Mrs Flynn?'

She nodded, and Maddy sighed. She had had a last hope that it might be a false alarm, that there were just contractions which might slow down and stop. No such luck. The waters had broken.

Ed had taken the usual readings, was now timing the contractions, trying to decide roughly when the baby might be born. Then he placed his hand on the woman's distended belly, gently palpated it.

Maddy was watching his face, saw the quick flash of alarm. He felt again. Then he said, 'Maddy, would you like to palpate?'

She did, and found at once what he was concerned about. This was something that she'd only read about, never experienced. Not that it was too uncommon, but it was to her. She managed to keep calm and said to Ed, 'Yes, I see.'

Ed stood back, peeled off his rubber gloves. 'Well, Mrs Flynn is certainly in labour. It's going to take quite a while before the actual birth, so you should be all right for an hour or two. Now, we are going to get things ready, if there's any sudden problem, phone us. Mr Flynn, on no account are you to leave the cabin. We still have people suffering from gastroentiritis, and we don't want it in here.'

'Is my baby going to be all right?' Mrs Flynn sobbed.

Ed's face softened and he nodded. 'I've never lost a newborn baby yet,' he said firmly. 'I don't see any problems. Now, try to stay calm because you'll need all your energy. We'll be back shortly.'

Maddy walked down the corridor with him. 'You've never lost a newborn baby because you've never delivered one outside hospital,' she said.

'I lied, Maddy. I have lost a baby.' A short, flat state-ment, delivered without emotion. Ed went on, 'But we had to reassure Mrs Flynn. Now, what did you feel when you palpated?'

Maddy was shocked by his statement that he had lost a baby, she wanted to know more. But yet again this was not the right time to ask. 'I've never felt one. But I thought the baby's head was in the wrong place. The baby is upside down—I mean the right way up. It's going to be a breech birth.'

'I think so, too. Can we cope with a breech birth?'

'We've got medical textbooks in the centre. Let's go and look it up.'

When they reached the medical centre they found the captain waiting for them. Maddy thought it typical—it might be the middle of the night, but the captain had dressed properly, formally. 'I need to know the situation, Doctor,' he said. 'Then I will make a decision. It'll be an informed decision as I will be guided by you. But the decision will be mine.'

Maddy saw that Ed approved of this attitude.

'We have a woman going into labour, about four weeks prematurely. There might be complications, though small ones. On shore I would recommend she be taken to hospital at once. Moving her from here by boat or helicop-ter could be dangerous. But, of course, it would no longer be your responsibility.'

Maddy smiled to herself, she knew Ed had slipped this in on purpose. She also knew what the captain's response would be.

'Everyone on this ship is my responsibility until they

are safe on shore. Can you and Maddy deal with these complications?'

'Probably. Any risk would be small.' Maddy thought it interesting to see how precise Ed was trying to be. 'But there is a risk. However, I have a suggestion.'

'Which is?'

'We have a very experienced midwife at Penhally Bay. There may be a storm raging but we also have fishermen there who could probably get her here.'

'Would she take that risk? It's a lot to ask.'

For a moment Ed was silent. Then he said, 'Perhaps not. Her husband died during a sea rescue some years ago. But I could always ask her.'

The captain thought a moment, then said, 'Will you try her, please? And make it clear, to her and the fisherman, that price is not a consideration.'

'The fisherman might need paying but Kate won't,' said Ed. He picked up the receiver, flicked on the speaker-phone and dialled.

Maddy was sitting next to Ed. She heard the phone ring, then heard a sleepy voice say, 'Kate Althorp here. Whose baby is being born in the middle of the night?'

'Middle of the night and the middle of the sea. Kate, it's Ed Tremayne here. I'm on the cruise ship.' His voice was a bit diffident, and Maddy guessed that he didn't know Kate too well.

'And you've got a birth out there?

'A primigravida, about four weeks premature. And a breech presentation.'

'How far is labour advanced?'

'I calculate at least three or four hours to go.'

'You need a midwife,' Kate said. 'And you're in luck. Jem is spending a fortnight at a friend's house.'

Ed winced. What a thing to forget! Kate had an eight-year-old son. Still, it turned out he wasn't a problem. 'So do you fancy coming? Kick Jerry Buchan out of bed and ask him to bring you here? His boat is the safest one for miles and there'll be good money for him.'

'That'll bring Jerry. I'll come.'

Maddy saw Ed hesitate. 'Kate, this is the worst storm for years. It's dangerous. Are you sure you want to...to risk it?'

There was a pause. Then a flat voice said, 'I'll risk it. Other people do. Other people have done. What kind of equipment have you got there?'

'We've plenty of high-class medical stuff. Drugs, bandages, sutures, instruments and so on. We've got a very well-equipped theatre you can use. Specific midwifery kit—none. It's not supposed to be needed.'

'I can bring what I need. I'm on my way. I'll be perhaps an hour, an hour and a half. Oh, and, Ed, tell the mother that she's probably going to have an awful backache and the best way to deal with it is to be on all fours.'

'I didn't know that. I'll tell her.' Ed replaced the receiver, looked at the captain. 'You heard that, Captain?'

The captain nodded. 'I'll have the lights on, and a good crew on the landing platform. And I'll be there.'

'Right.' Maddy saw Ed thinking. 'Maddy, we've still got the gastro to deal with. But for the moment I'll see to that. How about if you arrange to get Mrs Flynn transferred to one of the wards here—with her husband—and then keep an eye on her until Kate arrives?'

'Seems a good plan.' She was glad that as usual he had asked her instead of directing her.

'Let's get started. Captain, we'll keep you informed. But for the moment I feel happier.'

'I never had problems like this when I was Captain of one of Her Majesty's frigates,' the Captain said gloomily.

After arranging for Kate to come aboard, Ed had little to do but check up on mostly sleeping patients, see that the stewards were happy with their work. And they were. There were no more new cases, no sudden crises.

He felt responsible for bringing Kate out to the ship, so when he heard that the fishing boat was nearing the landing platform, he went out on deck. He knew that probably the most dangerous part of her trip would be the jump between fishing boat and platform. So he wanted to be there. Perhaps he might be able to help.

It took an effort to push open the door that led to the deck. And when he did step outside, the wind whipped across his face, pushing him violently against the railing.

He had lived by the sea for much of his life. But he had never seen, or heard, a storm like this. The waves were breaking as they did on the shore. There was the hiss of them as they smashed against the side of the ship. And above all the howl of the wind screaming through the ship's rigging.

He could make out the dancing lights of the fishing boat as it approached the landing platform. The landing platform itself was brightly lit, showing the chaos of waves beating at it. He'd asked Kate to come out in this! Just for a moment he wondered how he would feel if there was an accident. If Kate were injured—drowned even? What would his father say?

Interesting that he thought of his father first.

Then he decided that he was being foolish. Sometimes decisions had to be made. If necessary, he would make them.

He saw the captain approaching him, clutching the railings as he did so. 'Dr Tremayne? Not expecting to go down onto the platform, are you?'

'I wondered if I might be of help.'

'You'd only get in the way. My crew are trained. Leave them to do their job.'

Probably—certainly—true. He'd stay here, where he could do no harm. He noticed the captain did the same.

The fishing boat came alongside the platform, tossed by the waves so that sometimes the two were level and sometimes the boat was a good six feet lower. Ed saw a fisherman on the boat wave to one of the crew waiting on the platform and then throw a bag across. The crewman caught it, ran to take it to safety. The boat sank again below the platform level.

Ed saw two of the crew poised right on the edge of the platform. Each was fitted with a safety line, controlled by another crewman further back. Ed saw the boat rising— and there was Kate, balanced on the edge of the fishing-boat deck, a fisherman holding her from behind. A wave swept the fishing boat upwards, Kate jumped. She landed on her knees on the landing platform, where the two crewmen grabbed her.

She was safe. She was half hurried, half dragged back into the ship. The fishing boat stood off at once, with just a wave from the fisherman.

'A good competent job,' the captain said to Ed.

Ed wiped his forehead. It was cold out here—but he had been sweating.

A crewman brought Kate up to them, and the captain escorted her inside the ship. Then he said, 'I'm Captain Smith. Mrs Althorp, welcome aboard. I don't need to tell you how thankful I am to have you here, I think you know. Anything you need, just ask for. Now I'll leave you to Dr Tremayne.'

Ed smiled his relief. 'I'll keep my distance from you, Kate, just in case, but you don't know how glad I am to see you. I know it was a lot to ask.'

'Because of my husband being killed in a storm?'

He had not expected her to be as forthright as this. 'That's right. You must have been terrified.'

She shook her head. 'Not so. This is my way of fighting back.'

'Good. And you're not too tired to work?'

Kate looked at him sardonically. 'Since when did babies come only in the daytime? Midwives are on twenty-four-hour call. Anyway, how are you coping with this outbreak Nick told me about?'

He shrugged. 'We're coping. There's a nurse here.'

'So I heard. Is one nurse enough? How good is she?'

'She's very good. We've bonded, we're a team, she knows what I want before I do.'

He felt Kate look at him again. 'So quickly,' she commented casually. 'What is she like as a person?'

He had wondered about this and then decided that this wasn't the time or place for any such thoughts. 'She's professional,' he said, 'which is all I need right now.'

'Of course,' Kate said.

CHAPTER FIVE

STILL keeping his distance, Ed took Kate to the medical centre. Then he told her to go inside, introduce herself to Maddy and the mother, and do what was necessary. 'There's clean scrubs available, you'll want to get out of those wet clothes. You're in charge, Kate. Maddy will give you a buzzer, you can contact me if you need me.'

Kate nodded. 'I'll probably need you when we deliver. It might be an idea to have both of you. But before you get inside my delivery room, you make sure you're clean!'

'Shower and new scrubs on us both,' he promised her. Then he set off on his rounds again.

Maddy joined him fifteen minutes later. When he saw her smiling at him he felt his spirits lift. It was good to see her, even though it had only been a couple of hours since he'd seen her last. Why do I feel this way? he wondered. Then he decided it was just a side effect of fatigue.

'How have you got on with Kate?' he asked.

'Wonderfully. She inspires instant confidence, doesn't she? Are all the members of your practice like that?'

'Of course. Do I inspire instant confidence?'

She pursed her lips. 'I'm afraid you do. But I still have

to be convinced that it's genuine medical ability and not just a con trick.'

'It was a weekend course I went on, just for GPs. How to inspire instant confidence and thus cheer up patients even if they are dangerously ill. Is Kate happy with her patient?'

'Very happy. And the patient is happy, too. Even Mr Flynn is happy. Kate took him to one side and gave him a short but intense lecture on the duties and functions of a father-to-be in a delivery room.'

'Kate has her own way of doing things,' Ed said.

'I'm glad that she's come,' Maddy said after a pause. 'But if it hadn't been possible, could we have managed on our own?'

Ed thought for a moment. Then he said, quite honestly, 'Together we would have been fine. But I'm not sure I could have managed. It's not something I'd want to do on my own.'

His face went blank and just for a moment Maddy had the impression that some memory had returned to haunt him. And she remembered how earlier he had said that he had lost a baby. But then he smiled and said, 'Anyway, the problem's over now. I think we have a good team.'

'We do,' Maddy said.

Together they looked in at six patients, had quiet conversations with the stewards. The lull was continuing. But they still had to work and they knew that nearer morning, things would get worse.

'Aren't you tired yet?' she asked him. 'You only had an hour's sleep.'

'It refreshed me. And a situation like this brings its own momentum. It drags you along with it. But how about you? Aren't you tired? You've had no sleep at all.'

'I'm fine,' she told him. Then she said something that suggested that she was not as in control as she'd thought. 'And I really like working with you.'

There was a pause, a long pause. 'It's mutual. I really like working with you,' he said eventually. 'I think you're a very fine nurse.'

She thought that she would have liked something a little more personal than that.

But it was a start.

His buzzer sounded. He listened to the message and said, 'I see. We'll be right there.'

'Mr Simmonds,' he said to Maddy. 'Remember my father was worried about him? I've dropped in to see him a couple of times, he's not doing too well.'

'He was one of the first to fall ill. He didn't send for me like the others. One of the stewards asked me to call round. When I called in he didn't complain, just said that these things happen, that we had to put up with them.'

'Hmm. A fatalist. Anything more you know about him?'

'He kept very much to himself, didn't look for company. Apparently he booked this trip six months ago with his wife—but she died three months later. He told me that they had planned the trip together so he was going to come on it in memory of her.'

She thought Ed looked uneasy. 'That seems an odd thing to do to me,' he said. 'However, let's see how he is.'

They went to the cabin and Maddy knew at once that

things weren't good. Neither the drip nor the drugs had been able to control his fever. His skin was hot and dry, and he was shivering. His temperature was far, far too high, and he was delirious. 'Biddy,' he mumbled, 'is that you, Biddy?'

'Who's Biddy?' Ed asked, though Maddy suspected he knew the answer.

She pointed to a photograph by the head of the bunk. It showed a younger Mr Simmonds and a laughing woman by his side. Looking as if they didn't have a care in the world. 'That's Biddy. She was his wife.'

Ed took up the photograph and stared at it. Then he replaced it, shook his head and when he spoke his voice was unnaturally calm. 'We've done all we can. It's up to Mr Simmonds now. Do you want to wait with him, make sure he's comfortable?'

Maddy knew her voice was shrill. 'What about trying the mammoth injection? Like you did for Mrs Jones? It worked for her. She's recovering.'

'It wouldn't work for this man.' Ed shook his head. 'He wouldn't survive it. Look, I'll leave you here for a while and check on some of the other patients. When it happens—and it won't be long—then buzz me.'

And he was gone.

Mr Simmonds died quietly, and Maddy wondered if there was a smile on his face. Certainly he looked at peace. And before she had time to buzz Ed he came back into the room. 'Mr Simmonds is dead,' she told him. 'Just as you said would happen.' She couldn't keep a thread of anger out of her voice.

His voice was gentle. 'I've seen a lot of deaths through

gastroenteritis,' he said, 'which is unusual, I know. In the West it's usually not a killer, whereas in the developing countries it often is. You learn in time to tell just who will survive and who won't. It's a feeling rather than a medical technique.'

'I thought you didn't like feelings. But you say that you've seen a lot of deaths through this. How many is a lot?' Her voice was abrupt. For some reason she had to keep pushing him. He had upset her.

He didn't reply at first, but then he said, 'A lot is over two hundred deaths in three weeks through gastroenteritis. That's not counting those who died for other reasons.'

Maddy winced. How could he carry on having seen so many deaths? Perhaps this was the time to back off. 'I'm sorry,' she said. 'And, Ed, before, I was a bit…a bit personal. I'm sorry.'

Perhaps there was a touch of humour in his voice. 'You don't have to be sorry. I like straight talking. Now I'd better pronounce death. Do we tell the captain now or let him have some sleep?'

'We ought to tell him, but there's absolutely nothing he can do. Let him sleep a little longer.'

Ed looked at Mr Simmonds's still form, looked at Maddy. 'Are you all right, Maddy?'

'I'm a nurse, I've seen death before. Don't worry about me, Ed.' She was glad they were OK again. 'Now I'll have to—'

Her buzzer sounded. Kate's voice said, 'Things are moving faster than I had expected here. Want to come and lend a hand? And can you get Ed to come, too? Is it possible?'

'He's here with me. We're both on our way.'

'Make sure you've showered, scrubbed yourselves and put on something clean. I like my delivery room sterile.'

'Right,' Maddy said.

They left Mr Simmonds's cabin, locking the door behind them.

Breech births were often faster than normal births, Maddy learned. The ideal position was supported squatting, which made it easier to perform an episiotomy.

The second stage occurred just as it was described in the textbooks. As it was a breech presentation it seemed to be faster than normal. The mother cried out one last time as Kate's capable hands busied themselves. Then Maddy saw the midwife smile.

'It's a little girl!' And then they heard that first tiny cry.

The parents had opted not to be told the baby's gender in advance.

Kate wrapped the little pink form in a blanket, clamped then cut the cord. She offered the wailing bundle to Ed so he could give her to her mother, to be put straight on the breast.

Ed shook his head, stepped back and indicated that Maddy should hand over the baby.

Maddy was happy to do it. She thought it was a magical moment when a mother saw her child for the first time. Unlike a lot of medicine, childbirth usually produced a happy ending. And as ever, the mother was overwhelmed, the pain now largely forgotten as the reward was so great.

'Have you thought of a name yet?' she asked Mrs Flynn.

She smiled weakly, exhausted but euphoric. 'No. We were going to wait and see what we got. No good picking a name if you're not going to use it, is it? But I think I'd like something to do with the sea.'

'We'll all have a think,' Maddy promised with a smile.

There was still the placenta to be delivered, the Apgar score to be recorded and Mrs Flynn checked for excessive bleeding. But although it had been a breech birth it had been largely trouble-free.

'Think you could have managed it?' Maddy whispered to Ed as Kate busied herself with her tasks.

'Not on my own. But I think perhaps that we could have managed it together. Though I think you would have been better at it than me. But in medicine it's always when you think that you can more or less manage that things go seriously wrong. Like I said, hope for the best, prepare for the worst.'

'There's the planning mind again. That's your slogan, isn't it? And I suppose it's quite a good one.' Maddy looked across the little theatre. 'Kate, I'll stay but do you need Ed any more?'

'No. But, Ed, once you've been out in that corridor, exposed to things, just to be on the safe side you're to keep out of the baby's ward. From now on it's an isolation ward. In fact, you keep out too, Maddy. Mother and baby are now my concern, I don't need you.'

'Bossy people, midwives,' Ed said.

They had decided that the mother and baby should be moved from the theatre to one of the small wards. Kate had already prepared it. She had also arranged for food to be delivered, for Mr Flynn to get what was necessary from their cabin and for him to have somewhere to sleep.

'You go and do the rounds,' Maddy suggested to Ed.

'Come back when we've got mother and baby settled and we'll have a drink to celebrate.'

'Champagne at half past five in the morning?'

'I thought that tea might be more sensible.'

'Then I'll be there.' Ed went to congratulate the mother again and left the room.

He came back three-quarters of an hour later to join Kate and Maddy. Kate had been given the now absent doctor's cabin. Mother and baby had been settled next door but an alarm ran from the ward to the cabin.

'Celebratory tea,' Maddy offered, 'and a special meal of chocolate biscuits.'

'Sounds good.'

'We'll have our little party and then Kate can sleep here for a while. Someone dragged her out of bed in the middle of the night.'

'I'll just doze,' Kate said, 'so I can listen out for my patients.'

Ed accepted a mug of tea and a chocolate biscuit. 'You didn't tell my father you were coming out here, did you?' he asked Kate.

Kate grinned at him. 'I did not. And you didn't ask him either, or he'd have been at the harbourside with a few things to say about the idea. He likes to be kept informed, so he's not going to be very pleased when you tell him.'

'That's something I'll have to deal with. Did you mind coming out here without his permission? Will he be angry at you?'

'Nick has been angry with me in the past—and I've been angry at him,' Kate said serenely. 'Somehow we've both got over it.'

Maddy couldn't quite make out the expression in Kate's eyes when she spoke about Nick. It wasn't just affection, there was a feeling of…wistfulness? Then she shrugged. It was the middle of the night, and Kate was obviously tired.

'What about a name for baby Flynn?' she asked. 'The mother thinks she'd like something to do with the sea.'

'The obvious one is Marina,' Kate said promptly. 'Or there are variations. Maris or Marnie or Rina.'

'I quite like Marina,' Maddy said. 'Are there any other sea-type names?'

'Dorian means child of the sea.' Kate was obviously an expert on names.

Maddy winced. 'You couldn't send any child out into the world called Dorian Flynn.'

Kate shook her head. 'Parents can do anything. Thank goodness this was a little girl. If it had been a boy, they might have called him Errol.'

Maddy had seen this happen before after a birth or a successful operation. If the staff had time they would sit together feeling excited, successful. They might have a half-joking conversation, like this, it was all part of sharing. And for the first time in some hours she was feeling relaxed.

'I want a baby some time,' she said. 'There was a time when I thought it was possible, when I could see a future with a husband and a baby, living in a house with a nice garden. I even bought a book of names. I rather fancied calling my daughter Hannah or my son Luke. But it never happened.'

'Plenty of time yet,' said Kate. 'Your chance will come.'

'Perhaps. Or perhaps I'll concentrate on my career and finish up the matron of a vast hospital.'

'Matron? You mean Senior Manager,' Kate snorted. 'Whatever that might be.'

Although he was sitting there, a half-smile on his face, Ed wasn't joining in the conversation. He didn't share in the excitement, the elation. Perhaps he was tired, Maddy thought. But, then, they were all tired.

Ed's buzzer sounded. He took the call, and Maddy heard him say, 'You were right to call me, I'll be right there.' He looked at Maddy. 'Mrs Gillan, cabin D35. The steward says she's very weak, panicking a little. I'll go and see how things are.'

'I'll come, too,' Maddy said. 'And Kate can stay here and doze.'

In fact, Mrs Gillan was over the worst of the infection. Her fever was down. But she was very tired, still afraid, more in need of reassurance than anything else. Ed examined her, told her that she was over the worst and gave her something to help her sleep. Then he said that he and Maddy would stay with her for a while. He chatted to her but Maddy thought that his usual good humour wasn't there, his words seemed a bit forced. Perhaps she should join in the conversation…

'We've just delivered a baby,' she told Mrs Gillan. 'Not what you expect on a cruise ship—but these things happen.'

Mrs Gillan looked vaguely interested. 'I'm expecting my first grandchild in two months,' she murmured. 'I'm quite excited.'

'It's something lovely to look forward to,' said

Maddy. 'Now, close your eyes and think of babies' names like we did.'

Shortly afterwards Mrs Gillan was sound asleep but Ed showed no wish to move from her cabin. Maddy looked at him, concerned. 'You seem a bit low,' she said. 'Is going without sleep getting to you?'

'I don't need sleep, Maddy. I'm fine.'

She noticed that he didn't deny that his spirits were low. 'Mrs Gillan here is fine and we've just had a very nice surprise with baby Flynn. The successful birth of a baby is usually one of the more enjoyable bits of medicine.'

'So I understand.'

'You understand? Is that all? Ed, what is the matter with you? In the past couple of hours you've changed. Something is hurting you—can't you tell me what? We've shared a lot so far. Can't you share this?'

His voice was bleak. 'All right, I'll share, though it's not something that usually I like doing. I'll tell you but I don't want to talk about it afterwards. Is that OK?'

She felt that she'd achieved something with him. A barrier between them was coming down. 'That's fine,' she said.

They were talking in whispers as they didn't want to disturb Mrs Gillan. 'You guessed I'd been in the army and I've told you that I worked in Africa, that I super-vised a so-called hospital where there was an epidemic of gastroenteritis.'

'I know that,' she said. 'It must have been horrific. How could you cope? And how do you cope now?'

'Same answer to both questions. Because I'm a doctor, it's what we do.' He paused, and she wondered what might come next, what could come next.

'It's the feeling of inadequacy,' he said. 'The anger at knowing that with a little more help you could do so much good. People around me were dying for the want of a few pounds' worth of drugs. Especially children. I started off strong, determined to do what I could and knowing that I'd have to be satisfied with doing my best. But it was a poor best. And as the days passed and I got more and more tired and the death rate didn't go down…well, it hurt. When I left that place I vowed that never again would I go back to an epidemic like it. But when I heard of this outbreak, I just had to come to see if I could cope.'

'But you're doing a fantastic job!' She frowned and said, 'But the memories are hurting, aren't they?'

'Something like that.'

She thought over what he had told her. 'But there's more isn't there?'

The answer came back too quickly to be true. 'No!'

There was silence for a moment and then she said, 'I'm interfering again, I know. But, please, would you tell me more about it some time? It would help me to know you better and I…I want to do that.'

Another long silence and she stared at his forlorn face. Then he took one of her hands, squeezed it and then somehow managed to smile. 'You're the only person I've ever been tempted to talk to about it. Perhaps some day I will tell you. But now you stay here with Mrs Gillan while I go to check on a couple more patients.' And he was gone.

Maddy made a quick nurse's check on Mrs Gillan and then sat down to think about what Ed had told her. Now she could understand him better. Every moment he had been on board he must have been reminded of that camp in Africa. She knew about battlefield trauma but she realised there was similar trauma for those who were not actually fighting.

Now she knew so much more about his life. Only she had a feeling that he had held something back. And that he wanted to tell her, but he couldn't let himself.

The next question was why did she want to know more about him? She'd already decided that he wasn't the kind of man she ought to care for. She didn't really want to care for any man. Or did she?

She remembered their kiss. How many hours ago had it been? Six, seven? Had it been as long as that? She had thought about it so often since. He had kissed her— without any encouragement at all. No encouragement? Well, she had put her hand on his arm. In a sense she had made the first overture. Just a little one, though.

There was the gentlest of taps on the cabin door then Ed came in. She looked at him almost in surprise, as if he was the last person she had expected. She had just been thinking about him!

'If Mrs Gillan's OK, I could do with a hand on the next deck,' he said quietly.

'She's asleep and she'll stay that way. I'm coming.'

They walked out of the cabin, along the deserted companionway, They came to a porthole, and for a moment both stopped to look at the dark raging sea outside.

Once again, she put her hand on his arm. 'You have to know I'm not like this,' she said. 'I'm off men, I don't want any new relationship, I don't really even know you. But we agreed. This is time out. We're on a ship, what we do here doesn't count. So I want you to kiss me again. Just for comfort, for you as well as me.' She stopped a moment, looked up at him and asked hesitantly, 'That is, if you want to kiss me.'

She could tell that he did want to kiss her. One arm round her waist, one hand holding the back of her head, gently he leaned towards her. When their bodies were touching it felt so…so right. As if she were coming home, as if she belonged here. And there was no hurry. She wrapped her arms round his waist.

He was stroking her, his fingertips caressing the soft skin of her throat and cheek. It was gentle but it felt so good.

Then his lips touched hers. Softly at first, then, when she offered no resistance, harder, stronger, more demanding. What had started as gentle, cautious turned into something far more desperate, more passionate. She could feel her need for him growing within her. Suddenly her breasts were taut, her body feeling a warmth that had nothing to do with the air around them. And she knew he felt it, too, his need was all too obvious. And she liked it. Perhaps they could…

And then he eased them apart. She whimpered softly, she didn't want him to go. His reluctance was obvious, too. So why was he doing this?

They stood facing each other, heads down, linked only by their still clasped hands. Her voice trembling, she said, 'Remember, this is not serious. It's a time apart, we're both weary, we needed respite. It was so good—but it stops here.'

'As you wish,' he agreed. 'We'll forget it happened— or try to. Now, we have patients to look at.'

She was confused, saddened a little. Did he have to agree so readily?

* * *

An hour before dawn Ed told her to go to bed. 'You're flagging,' he said gently. 'You've worked hard and now you need a break. Maddy, don't argue, go to bed and sleep. I can cope.'

'But you need—'

'I need you refreshed and alert, so go to bed. I can spare you for three hours.'

She couldn't help it, she yawned. 'All right. I will go,' she said, 'providing you promise to wake me after exactly three hours.'

'I promise. I need you.'

She saw that he meant it and it made her feel good.

She went to her cabin, decided to do as he had and have a quick shower. Then she heard movements from next door, wrapped a towel round herself and peered into the corridor. There was Kate, coming out of the little ward. 'Everything all right?' Maddy asked.

'Everything is fine. Though I'd like to get off this ship. It's not the right place for a newborn. But mother's doing well, the baby's going to be called Marina and I've spent a fair amount of time reassuring the husband. It's a good thing that men don't have to have babies!'

'You're not the first midwife I've heard say that.' Maddy yawned again. 'Ed's sent me to bed. Just for three hours.'

'That man is a good doctor. Sometimes he reminds me of his dad, sometimes not.'

'So you and Nick are good friends?'

'We've known each other for years.'

Maddy thought there was a peculiar inflection in Kate's

voice, but perhaps she was tired. 'So, bed for me,' she said. 'Goodnight.'

'Good morning.' Kate grinned.

The minute Kate got into her bunk she realised that she was sleeping in the same sheets that Ed had slept in. Mind you, he had slept in the sheets that she had… What did it matter? These weren't easy times. But she thought she could detect just the faintest smell…as if his warm body were still in the bed. The thought excited her.

Ed Tremayne. Eighteen hours ago she had never met him. Now they were colleagues, friends even. He had kissed her twice and she had enjoyed it, much to her surprise. She had to stop thinking! Ed Tremayne was just…

She had only just shut her eyes—she thought. But there was a gentle hand on her shoulder and an enticing smell of coffee. Eyes still closed, she asked, 'Three hours?'

'To the minute,' came Ed's voice. 'There's coffee by your bed and…oh, there's a message for you sent down from the radio office. Now I'll leave you to get dressed.'

She opened her eyes then stared at him. He seemed entirely undisturbed by his night awake. Perhaps the lines around his eyes were a little deeper, but he still looked confident, in charge of the situation.

She sat up. Then she remembered that when she had gone to bed she hadn't bothered with a nightie. Hastily, she scrambled under the sheets again. But not before she had seen the gleam of appreciation in his eyes.

'I'll go and talk to Kate until you're ready,' he said. 'Or, more likely, I'll shout down the corridor at her so as to keep things sterile. See you when you're ready.'

She drank half her coffee and then reached for the message. Who could it be from? She'd never had a cable before.

Her morning was spoiled at once—the message was from ex-boyfriend Brian. Why couldn't he leave her alone? She skimmed the contents, though she knew what they'd be. *I can't believe what you said to me... Remember what we had? Remember you telling me you loved me? This will go on for ever...I love you and that is all that matters... Need to get together so we can sort things out... You know you'll have to see me... I'll get a job and then... Madeleine, I am serious...*

The message was timed—how could he have sent a message at three that morning? Then she remembered that one of the things he did was to sleep during the day and contact her in the middle of the night. Just because he felt like it.

She felt resentment and fear welling up in her. This was what happened when you put your trust in men. In love. One sad thing was that she did remember what they'd had. It had been so good and it had turned out so bad.

So, back to her resolve. No more contact with men. Then she thought about Ed. Like Brian, he was determined, too. But Ed was different. He could see another person's point of view. Couldn't he?

She screwed up the message, slid it into her bedside cabinet. Then she finished her coffee, though it didn't seem so good now. She dressed and then felt the beginnings of a slight headache. Strange, she hadn't had one before. Still, there was work to be done.

She found Ed in the corridor. He turned to her and smiled but she couldn't work up any enthusiasm to greet him. 'What do you want me to do now?' she asked.

She might have guessed—he detected her change in mood at once. 'Are you sure you're all right?' he asked. 'You seem a little out of sorts.'

'There's nothing wrong with me,' she snapped. 'I've just got a job to do.'

'Not bad news from your message?'

'I told you, Ed, I'm fine, really. The message was from…an old friend. He wants to get in touch. Perhaps I'm just a bit tired still.'

But she knew he didn't believe her.

They worked steadily for the next four hours and after a while she thought she saw some progress. Just a little, not much. Fewer people were now falling sick. One or two of the first to fall ill now appeared to be recovering. It was encouraging—just.

They were still a good team but the old camaderie with Ed had gone. The message from Brian had scared her. She knew that no one could be less like Brian than Ed. But she had decided to abandon all hopes of an emotional relationship with a man and Brian's call had reawakened this decision. So she and Ed worked well together, but there was no longer the old feeling of joy in their joint work.

They ate when they could, apparently surviving on a diet of coffee and chocolate. And then, midmorning, Ed said, 'I think we can take a fifteen-minute break. Things are easing up. We've been spending too much time in sick-rooms and air-conditioned corridors. We need real air. We'll go on deck for a while.'

So they went on deck and it was exhilarating. The waves were breaking against the ship's hull and the wind was as strong as ever. A gust made her stagger, and he put his arm around her back to steady her. It was just a friendly gesture, but his arm felt warm and strong and she liked it. And it seemed to stay there a little longer than was strictly necessary.

'Look,' he said, pointing to where there was a little gathering of white buildings on the coastline. 'That's Penhally Bay.' Then he pointed to a little boat being bounced about in an alarming fashion by the waves. 'See that fishing boat? Well, I'll bet my father's on it. It'll be Jerry Buchan bringing him out, the man who brought Kate last night.'

'Is it a good idea, coming out in this weather?'

Ed grinned ruefully. 'Probably not a good idea. And he could have done everything necessary by phone. But being Nick Tremayne, he has to come out in person. Especially as Kate is here.'

'And you respect him for it, don't you?'

'I suppose I do. And I also suppose that in his shoes I'd have done the same thing. Look, he won't be long getting here. Let's go down to the landing platform and meet him.'

As before, they were told by the crew to wait safely on deck, while crewmen helped Nick out of the wildly pitching fishing boat and up the steps towards them. Then Maddy witnessed the apparently emotionless meeting between the two men.

'How's the job going, Ed?'

'We're coping. We've had two deaths, one unrelated.'

'Right. You're tired?'

'I'm still on top of things.'

A curt nod from his father. 'What I would have expected. Now, I've got to see the captain. Want to come with me?'

'Maddy comes, too,' said Ed. 'This has been a joint effort.'

'Of course she comes, too. Now, let's go.'

Maddy wondered if the two knew just how much they were alike. She also wondered if they ever showed the deep love that she suspected was between them. For the Tremayne family, it seemed that emotions were to be kept strictly under control. But she was sure they were there.

But was it her business? Did she want to know more about Ed's emotions?

CHAPTER SIX

NICK knew that probably it shouldn't have been, but his first thought was for his son. Nick was one of the few men who could guess what Ed had just been through. Who could guess what hurt he must have felt. A gastroenteritis outbreak. The sights, the smell, the sounds, all must have come crashing back on him. Not a lot of men could have stood that.

A small smile of paternal pride touched Nick's lips as he looked at his obviously weary son. Ed might be weary but he was confident and he was in charge of the situation. He was a Tremayne. Of course, Nick was not going to say anything. But he was proud of his son.

They were now sitting in the captain's cabin. They were handed coffee and then the captain said, 'I've been in touch with our head office and with Dr Tremayne here. Dr Tremayne, I'd like you to review the situation.'

Nick said, 'I've been phoned by the relevant port authorities, and the ship must remain in quarantine for another forty-eight hours at least. Yesterday, last night and this morning I worked on trying to identify the cause of the disease. Ed was right. It is bacterial in origin, not a virus. But it's a completely new strain, a very powerful one, there'll be a lot of people taking an interest in it. Still, this makes no difference to the treatment. Now, I've come here in person to look around, help if possible and then accompany my midwife back to shore. The midwife I didn't know had come out here.'

He looked severely at Ed, who looked serenely back.

Nick went on, 'The Met Office has said that the gale has almost blown itself out and conditions should rapidly improve. The navy has offered to help. They've liaised with the cruise line and later this afternoon one of the navy's smaller boats will come and take off the new baby and her parents. At the same time they'll bring out a small team of nurses and another doctor.'

'Who's the other doctor?' asked Ed.

'A Dr Wyatt. Apparently she's not long out of medical school, but she gained an excellent pass.'

'What is her experience of dealing with an epidemic?'

'As far as I know, none at all,' Nick said flatly. 'I didn't procure the doctor. The cruise line did.'

'This isn't work for a new doctor.' Ed said. 'I think I should stay in charge for a while longer.'

There was a silence and then the captain said, 'I would like you to stay. It'd be foolish to change responsibilities in the middle of the situation. As head of the practice, do you agree, Dr Tremayne?'

'I do,' Nick said after a short pause. 'Ed should stay a while longer. You can arrange this with the line?'

'The line left me without a doctor—and look what happened. They'll do whatever I say.'

'Right. In that case, Captain, I'll go down to see how I

can help in the medical centre. I'd really like to take a good look at this new baby.'

'Keep me informed of everything,' the captain warned.

As soon as they reached the centre Maddy was called away. Kate was asleep, and Nick decided not to wake her up. For the first time since he'd boarded the ship he was alone with his son. And there were things he wanted to say to him.

'You should have consulted me before bringing Kate out here in the storm,' he said reproachfully. 'Surely you know about her husband being drowned? How do you think she felt?'

'I thought she might have been terrified but, in fact, I don't think she was. But terrified or not, I would have wanted her here. She was the best available person for the job so I asked her to come. You'd have made exactly the same decision, wouldn't you?'

'I still would have liked to have been consulted,' Nick said, avoiding the answer he knew he'd have had to give. 'Couldn't you have managed without her?'

'Possibly. Probably. But she made a better job of it than either Maddy or I could have done. It was safer to have her there. Why don't you ask her what she felt about being called out in a storm?'

'I don't need to.' Nick scowled. 'I know exactly what she'd say.' Then he smiled. 'I like to have good people working for me. Now, how're you getting on with Maddy?'

'She's a brilliant nurse,' Ed said, turning away for the moment and rummaging through a pile of forms. 'We've worked well together.'

'Just a brilliant nurse? I thought I saw some attraction there between you.'

'I like her. But I don't do attraction. I've been married once and that's enough for me. I doubt I'll ever see her again when I leave the ship.'

'I see,' said Nick.

'I've got a patient I want to look at now,' Ed went on. 'Kate's in the second cabin down the corridor. Why don't you go and give her a shake? She'll take you to see Sarah and Marina Flynn. You know she'll be mad at you if she finds out you've been here for a while and not woken her.'

'Good idea,' Nick said.

He waited until his son had left and then went into the corridor. There was Maddy taking something from a store cupboard. 'You need something, Nick?' she asked. He thought she looked flushed. Tired? Or upset?

'Ed's gone to see to a patient,' Nick said. 'We were having a chat when I saw you pass outside. He didn't see or hear you. It just struck me that you might have heard something of our conversation.'

'Nick, I do not eavesdrop! I heard a mumble, that was all.'

He lifted his hands placatingly. 'Of course not.' But he was an experienced doctor and he knew when people weren't telling the entire truth.

'In fact, I was telling him that I thought I'd seen an attraction between the two of you. He said he didn't do attraction, that he'd been married once. He doubts he'll ever see you again after he leaves this ship.'

'I'm sure that's true,' Maddy said, turning away. 'As for attraction, well, we work well together, that's all. Like I worked well with you.'

Whatever feelings she had seemed to be under control, Nick thought. And he had always tried to make it a rule never to interfere with the personal lives of his children. Whenever he had broken that rule and interfered, it had never worked out. But… 'Ed and I have been apart a lot,' he said. 'We've never been really close, which is a pity. But he is my son. Perhaps I know how he feels, and I think you mean a bit more to him than he realises.'

There, that was it, he had said it. He could do no more.

'I doubt that's true,' Maddy said in an offhand voice. 'He's off relationships and I certainly am.'

But Nick could tell that she was pleased—or at least intrigued.

Nick was alone in the medical centre now. He wandered around, admiring the fittings, peering into the ward where the mother and new baby were peacefully sleeping. He wanted a closer look at them—but not until he was with Kate. And then he went into the cabin where he had been told Kate was asleep.

There was a low light left on by the head of the bed, partly illuminating Kate's face, making it a thing of planes and shadows. She was a handsome woman. He had known her since his youth, so many years ago. And now he was having difficulty in reconciling the mature woman he was looking at with the teenager he had once known.

It wasn't like him. Usually he was certain, knew what to do, what to think. But now he wasn't sure. Possibly it was the storm outside but it brought back memories of that evil night when the Penhally lifeboat had been launched and Kate's husband, James, and Nick's own brother and father had all died during the rescue of a party of school-children. So much had happened that night, so many emotions, of grief and fear and despair. Intense emotions that had overwhelmed Kate and himself that fateful night. Leading to something that had never been acknowledged by either of them since.

Kate and he went back a long time. They had been teenagers together, with that fizzing off-on relationship that was so common in the young. But then life had come between them. He went to university and married Annabel, she had married James. Both Annabel and James were now dead.

Was Kate happy? he wondered. She seemed serene enough as she went about her work. Was he happy? That was a question he, a busy GP, shouldn't even try to answer. In fact, he shouldn't even ask it.

He and Kate were colleagues—friends, he supposed. But they were wary of each other. Sometimes he caught her looking at him and he wondered what she thought.

He slipped into the cabin, sat on a chair and looked at her. It had been years since the storm. He had fought against thinking of that night, had tried to push it out of his mind, certainly never mentioned it. But now he did think of it. And the memory was as vivid as if it had all happened yesterday.

For a while he didn't want to do anything. He was content just to sit there, to gaze at her sleeping face. But it didn't last long. Perhaps the very intensity of his gaze was felt by her. He saw her eyes twitch open and then focus.

'Nick! What are you doing here?'

'I had to see the captain, sort out a few things. And I

wondered about you. I wanted to see if one of my staff was all right.'

It was important to emphasise that he was concerned because she was a member of his staff. Safer that way.

'I would have liked to have been more involved last night,' he went on. 'I should have been told.'

Kate was as practical as ever. 'I left you a note explaining things and details of who would handle my work today. There was no need for you to go without sleep.'

'Perhaps not.'

Unlike Ed and Maddy, Kate had not bothered to undress when she'd lain down on the bunk. Now she sat up, waved at Nick. 'Wait outside for me. I need a couple of minutes to freshen up. I take it you've come to look at Marina and Sarah Flynn?'

'Just a quick check.' Then he remembered that Kate was always particular about the relative functions of a doctor and midwife, so he added, 'If that's all right with you.'

'It is.'

'The storm seems to be dying down a bit. This afternoon we've got a navy boat coming alongside, bringing nurses and another doctor. They've offered to ship you, the baby and her mother back to Penhally Bay. What do you think?'

'They're both doing fine. I'd certainly like to get them off this ship.'

'Your decision.'

She seemed short with him, and he now realised why. He had seen her asleep, almost defenceless. And Kate always had her defences in place. 'I'll organise you a drink,' he said. And then, wanting to say something pleasant, something that might bring them a little closer together, he added, 'You've done brilliantly, Kate.'

'I know,' she said.

He was a doctor. He was a scientist who believed in empirical proofs, who disdained what he called the mumbo-jumbo of astrology, of sixth senses, of the supernatural. But for a moment he wondered if what he had been remembering had somehow communicated itself to Kate. He would really like to know.

A quick inspection and it was obvious that mother and baby were doing fine. In fact, they were thriving. So what was now most important was to get them away from the ship. Kate agreed that they should move out with the navy boat. 'Now you can go and help Ed,' she told Nick. 'I can cope here very well.' He thought that Kate could always cope. On her own.

Ed, glad of Nick's help, handed him a list. 'I've given you these fifteen people to check over,' he said. 'It's just a case of making sure that the right drugs are given, the right IVs set up. The stewards are pretty good now but it's as well to keep an eye on them. You know where everything is?'

'I'll manage,' said Nick.

It felt just a little unusual, taking orders from his son, but he knew that in a case like this there could only be one leader. And he had to admit that Ed was good at it. He looked as tough as ever—but his eyes were getting bloodshot. Maddy, too, was showing signs of fatigue. But Nick could tell that there was no way she would ask for respite. Not while Ed was still working.

The disease on ship was peaking. There were now forty-eight people on board infected with it. That was forty-eight people falling ill, being ill or recovering from illness. They needed constant care and attention. But they should all survive.

Then the news came down from the captain. The pinnace was on its way. And the storm had nearly blown itself out. Ed said, 'Dad, why don't you go and scrub up and then get ready to help Kate move the Flynns?'

'Good idea,' said Nick. 'When will I see you on shore again?'

A short answer. 'When I think my job's done.'

A good answer, too, Nick thought.

They all look clean, energetic and above all awake, Maddy thought. Whereas she felt weary, crumpled and apathetic. She had watched as the new medical team had come aboard, each carrying a small bag. She had watched as one of them had helped Kate and Nick transfer the Flynn family to the pinnace. She was glad the family had gone.

Now they were sitting, crammed into the medical centre, listening to Ed. Three nurses in uniforms. They were all about her own age but for some reason she felt older than them. And there was the young doctor, Dr Ellen Wyatt. Slim, pretty, vivacious. Maddy suspected she was just out of medical school. She was also suspicious of the way the young doctor looked approvingly at Ed. It was more than just professional curiosity. She had moved her seat deliberately to sit next to him.

And Maddy had to admit that Ed still looked good. So long without sleep didn't appear to have affected him too much. There were lines round his eyes—now bloodshot eyes. And his mouth was more grim than before. But he looked better than she felt.

She was sitting at the side of the room while Ed briefed the nurses and the doctor. He had arranged things with the captain and herself, organised cabins to sleep in, meals, treatments, the nurses' roster. She had been consulted but it was obvious that this was something that Ed was expert at. Even the captain had listened. Ed was a superb organiser. And he made it clear that he was in charge.

'If there are any nursing problems, first buzz Maddy. I'll not give her any cases, she will be on call here for the next few hours. If you need a doctor, buzz Dr Wyatt first. If necessary, she'll liaise with me. Now, there are times when you'll have to work fast. But, remember, you don't cut corners. And records are all-important! Don't let them slip.'

Then he smiled, and Maddy could feel the stirring of interest. 'Last thing, everyone. Thank you for coming at such short notice. Now! We have work to do!'

Maddy realised that in a weird way Ed was enjoying himself. He was forcing himself to the limit, losing himself in work. She now knew why. He was causing himself so much present pain to try to push past pain out of his mind.

Just for a moment she wondered what life would be like when this was all over. Would they ever see each other again—even casually? Would he move out of her life, forget her? As he had told his father he would do?

Or would she forget him? She had to be honest and admit it. She didn't think she would forget him. In fact, a life in which she didn't see something of Ed—it would be hard.

CHAPTER SEVEN

INEVITABLY there were problems but most of them were quickly sorted out. The new team didn't yet know where to find things, what the protocols were, what the right relationship with the stewards was. But they learned, and Maddy had to admit that they were conscientious, hardworking. She worked for a few hours. And then at midnight Ed came into the medical centre and said, 'Things are running smoothly now so you go to bed.'

Bed! She could think of few places she'd rather be. Taking the strain off her eyes, her legs, her back. Blissful just to lie there. 'All right,' she said. 'Aren't you going to sleep too?'

'I am. I've arranged with Dr Wyatt for her to take the next six-hour shift. If it's desperate she will wake me, but I doubt it will be necessary. I've got twenty minutes' more work to do then I'll sleep for those six hours, just as you are going to.'

'Right. And you're in the other nurse's cabin, which is next to mine?' For some reason, the question seemed very important to her.

'That's right. I'll sleep well there.'

'I'm tired but I won't sleep at once,' she told him. 'You know the stage when you've gone beyond being weary?'

He nodded, his eyes never leaving her face.

'Well, that's where I am. So instead of going straight to bed, I'm going to shower, wash my hair and then have a mug of tea with a shot of whisky in it. I feel like pushing the boat out a bit.'

She paused, afraid of the enormity of what she was going to say next. Staring at the floor, she said, 'If you want, you can come into my cabin and…have some tea and whisky, too.'

She felt his hand on her chin. With the most delicate of touches he lifted her head so they were looking at each other. He eyed her meaningfully, and unspoken messages passed between them. 'Are you sure?' he asked eventually.

'I'm sure. I'm certain. It's more than that, I want you to come for a drink with me.'

'Then I'd like to join you. Just for a while, of course.'

'Of course. I'll go now.' As she walked down the corridor she knew she had made a decision. Exactly what she had decided she didn't know.

She showered, shampooed her hair, and it was as wonderful as she had anticipated. She put on a clean nightie. Then she climbed into bed.

He knocked then came into her room twenty minutes later. 'Everything OK?' she asked.

'Everything is fine. They're a good team and I don't expect to be disturbed. You look…refreshed.'

'I am. Why don't you have a shower, too? There are spare towels in my bathroom.'

This was a lunatic conversation, she thought as he disappeared to shower. We're sidling round what we know we both want and neither of us dare say anything about it. Then she blinked, rethought things. Was this what she truly wanted? Or was she just blinded by fatigue? It wasn't too late to change her mind now.

Then she decided it was too late. Anyway, she knew what she wanted.

He came out of her bathroom, wearing only a towel wrapped round his waist. She winced as she saw scars on his naked chest. 'What are they?' she asked. 'You must have been terribly hurt.'

'Not too terribly. They're just flesh wounds. It's a danger that comes with being near a battlefield. Even if the war is unofficial.'

'I'd like you to tell me about it some time. But not now. I want to be calm and happy now.'

'Calm and happy. Sounds a good plan.'

She felt happy, but detached from herself. As if she could look down on what she was doing and judge it as an independent. She knew this was partly the result of fatigue. She also knew she'd want this even if she had slept all night and recovered.

They drank the tea she had made. He sat on the edge of her bed. 'You can sit there till you finish your drink,' she told him, 'but then you're to get in bed with me.'

He hesitated. 'Maddy, I do want to get in bed with you, desperately. But I don't want you to be hurt if...'

'I'll be hurt if you don't get in bed with me. Now, finish your drink.'

Was this her talking? she wondered. This just wasn't like her. She didn't do things like this, talk like this. She was throwing herself at a man—when she had promised herself that never again would she let a man take advantage of her. Well, it was done now. She'd made up her mind.

They sipped their drink in silence, finished almost together. She leaned over, switched off the overhead light so there was only the dim glow of the bedside lamp.

Now he was only a half-seen figure. He stood up and the towel round him dropped away. Another moment's hesitation, then he lifted the cover and slid into bed beside her.

She was really tired but in spite of this all her senses seemed extra-alert. She could hear and feel the hum of the shipboard machinery. She could smell the faint scent of whisky on his breath—or was it on hers? When he got closer to her she smelt the scent of her own soap. But it seemed different on him. Why would that be?

It was a bed rather than a bunk, but it was designed for one person. There was only just room for the two of them side by side. He didn't move or try to touch her, this seemed to be something that they had to do step by step. Perhaps it was her turn to do something. She wriggled upwards a little, crossed her arms and pulled her nightie over her head. Then she leaned across him to toss it carelessly onto the floor. As she did so she felt her breasts trailing over his naked chest. She smiled as she heard his sudden intake of breath.

When she was lying by his side again she let her fingers trail across him, gently touch the scar. 'Tell me more about this,' she said. 'There's a lot I don't know about you. And I want to know.'

She felt him shrug. 'It was an explosion. A mortar bomb lobbed into the camp hospital. A bit of white-hot metal gouged lumps out of me. It could have been a lot worse.'

'Which war was that?'

'No war had been declared. It was just people killing each other for no good reason.'

She could hear his bitterness, and decided it was better to move on to something else. 'Forget all that, I shouldn't have asked. But you're here with me now.'

His voice was urgent. 'Maddy, I am here with you now and it's wonderful but I don't know if we're doing the right—'

'You're trying to make sure that I know what I'm doing?'

'Yes.'

'Well, I do. Now, don't you really want to stay here with me?'

'Of course I do! But…'

'You've kissed me twice and it was wonderful. Both times we agreed that this was a thing apart, nothing serious, almost a shipboard romance. If you want, we'll carry on like that. For the moment that suits me.'

He said nothing. After a moment he slipped his arm around her shoulders and eased her back onto the pillow. 'Maddy, I—'

She laid a finger on his lips. 'We've gone beyond words. There are to be no promises, no confessions, no protestations. Let's face it, we're both damaged. We've both got pasts that hang over us. For now we'll forget the past and the concern that this could have no future. There's just the present, just you and me. And we can make each other happy. That would be so wonderful.'

Then she thought of something, something she should have thought of before. For a moment she was anxious. 'Last words—do you have precautions?'

He laughed. 'I stole something from your pharmacy. You have everything needed there.'

He leaned away from her, she heard the crackle of paper. For a moment she lay there, eyes closed, listening to the sound of his breathing. A last fugitive thought—was she making a mistake? But then he leaned over her, his face came down on hers and she closed her eyes.

She wasn't a virgin, of course, but neither was she vastly experienced. She was apprehensive now, her mind made up but not knowing what to expect. And Ed… She knew something of his character, how determined he was. What kind of lover would he be? Considerate, thoughtful, loving? He rolled onto his side, bent his head over hers and kissed her. A delicate kiss, his lips just touching hers. She had been kissed by him twice already. And the same magic worked as before. What started as something simple became suddenly something serious and exciting. It was still only his lips, her lips, meeting. Nothing more.

She was content for now—but where was he taking her? She was aware of his body, so close to hers and yet not touching. It was exciting. Tantalising. Now he leaned over her, his body above hers but still not touching. She could feel the warmth of him and knew that she had to do something. Reaching up, she slid her arms around him and eased him down so their bodies were now together, fully together. There seemed to be a lot of him. He seemed to cover her entire body, arms, legs, breasts all pressed against him. She felt that her body was owning his, he was paying the same tribute to her as she was paying to him.

They were still kissing. But the kiss was more passionate. And after a moment of bliss he took his lips from hers and kissed the rest of her face, her ears, the corners of her eyes, even the tip of her nose. Then he returned to her mouth again and she felt the strength of his desire as she met his probing tongue with hers.

He stopped, she whimpered, it had been so wonderful. Then he threw off the sheet that covered them. And his lips strayed downwards, touching the throb of the pulse in her neck, the edge of her arm and shoulder, the valley between her breasts. Then, after moments of almost unendurable expectation, he kissed her breasts. She moaned with ecstasy as he took each thrusting peak into his mouth. Her back arched, urging him onwards. It was the most exciting of caresses. She could feel it throughout her entire body, felt that dampness below that told her how ready, how quickened she was.

Now…he wasn't going to… He was… She sensed his head travel down her body, felt the touch of his tongue in that most secret of places. It made her cry out loud as he moved her towards a rapture she had never experienced before, never even dreamed of. Not long now.

Something told her that his need was as great as hers. Her hands slid down, grasped him and pulled him up to kiss her lips again. And her hips surged against his in silent longing and invitation.

It was so obvious, so perfect, like coming home. He was in her, part of her, they were joined body and spirit. A movement that both of them felt, a joint knowledge of something burgeoning, growing. It was something that could only be done when the two of them were together and then that moment of exaltation as they both cried out their pleasure.

Afterwards there was calm and contentment. She felt she could speak now. 'You are so good to me,' she murmured.

'And you are good to me, too,' he replied softly.

She slept through the night, the deep sleep of the completely exhausted. Then she half woke; she didn't know who she was, where she was, whose arm was round her. She only knew that she was warm, happy and safe, and that all the world was good to her. The man next to her would see to that. Perhaps she could sleep a little more and— A buzzer sounded and she was fully awake. Now she knew who, where and what she was. And who she was in bed with. But she was still happy.

Ed took his arm from under her, leaned out of bed and picked up the phone. 'Dr Wyatt? Of course not, I told you to… Yes, I'll be there in five minutes. Don't do anything until then.'

He rolled out of bed, she looked up at him and he bent over to kiss her. 'Maddy, I've got to work but…'

She held up her hand to stop him. 'It's OK, we don't need to talk about it. That way I'm certain there'll still be some…magic.'

He thought for a moment then nodded. 'Perhaps that is best. Carry on as if nothing had happened. But, Maddy, I think that—'

'Off you go! Back to your own cabin.' She glanced at the clock. They had had just over five hours' sleep. 'I'll be up soon and will come and help.'

He looked at her a moment, then turned to go.

She decided that she could stay in bed for a further fifteen minutes, but she knew she wouldn't sleep. She felt at a bit of a loss. He said they were to carry on as if nothing had happened. Was that the answer she really wanted? She wasn't sure.

She thought of yesterday and the time spent without sleep. She had worked harder than she had ever worked in her life before. She had been hounded by her ex-fiancé. She had watched the death of a man who had asked her to marry him. And she had slept with Ed and it had been wonderful. What more could the future bring? She didn't like to think. But there was no time to think now. She got out of bed.

The work went on. They now had two doctors and four nurses and assistance from the stewards. But Dr Wyatt and one of the nurses were taking a six-hour sleep break. And the work didn't get any less.

For some reason she didn't spend much time with Ed that morning. But they saw each other from time to time. She had been wondering just how the two of them would react when they were first working together again. All right, they had agreed to say nothing. But when they met it was impossible. There was an understood acknowledge-ment of what had happened, a special smile or a brief touch of hands, unrecognised by anyone else. It was only a little but it meant so much to her.

She was sneaking a quick lunch with one of the other nurses when Ed came and sat beside her. He had been in-sistent that they all have regular meals and had arranged for food to be brought to the medical centre. 'You need all the energy that you can get,' he had told them. 'Eat lightly but eat well.' And they had done so.

He sat opposite her, took a glass of orange juice and a plate of salad. Maddy felt uneasy as he looked at her. There was an expression on his face she didn't understand. Like nothing she had seen before. Fear? Horror? But his voice was calm as he said, 'I'd like you to come back with me when you've finished. I've got a case that's concerning me. Penny Cox. Do you know her?'

Maddy shook her head. 'No. I don't think she's ever been to the medical centre.'

'Probably not. She looks to be young, fit, apparently healthy. But she's had a splenectomy, the result of a motorcycle accident years ago.'

Penny Cox's condition had deteriorated, but she was strong and now Maddy was relieved to see that she seemed to be over the worst of it.

'I think she's OK now, Ed. I can call you if things change.'

Ed frowned. 'No, I'll stay, just to make sure she doesn't relapse. I'll be buzzed if I'm wanted.'

'Well, there's not too much I can do here. It's just a matter of waiting. Shall I go?'

He looked alarmed. 'No! No, I want you to stay. You can… You might be…'

It was then that she realised that there was more to this case than appeared. It meant something to him. 'Did you know this lady before?' she asked.

'No. Never met her before in my life. Never even heard of her.'

'It's just that…you seem especially interested in her. I know you've done your best for all of our patients, but this one seems to mean more to you than the others, you're more involved. Will you tell me why?'

It was the first time she had ever seen him at a loss, not been in absolute control of himself. He shook his head fretfully, then walked over and stared down at Penny Cox's white face.

Maddy wondered if she should walk over to him, perhaps put her arm around his waist to comfort him. She decided not to. Whatever demon he was wrestling with, he had to fight it on his own. But it was hard just to sit there, to know he was suffering.

The silence between them lasted for perhaps ten minutes, during which neither of them moved. And then there was a change. The only sound had been Penny's breathing, no longer heavy and laboured. Now Maddy felt she could go over to stand by Ed. 'Penny's over it, Ed,' she said. 'The worst has passed, now she stands a good chance of recovering.'

'I think you're right. This one stands a good chance of recovering.'

This one? Maddy thought. Who was he comparing her with?

She took his hand, and led him to the far side of the cabin. There was a bench there where they could sit together. Perhaps now was the right time. 'You're to tell me what's wrong,' she said, 'why you are suffering. You've given me hints but now I need to know everything. You told me about working in the hospital in Africa but I think there's more. I've already told you my story, told you things about my relationship with Brian that I've told no one else. Ed, we have to share. I know it's hard for you, you like to keep feelings locked up. But it's good to tell. And it's not bad to feel!'

He looked at her as if puzzled. 'Why are you so concerned about me, Maddy?'

'Because you're like me—you're carrying a load of memories that hurt. I'm offering you the chance to share that load.'

He still seemed puzzled, looking at her as if she had not fully understood him. 'But it's just not me to talk about things like that.'

'There are bits of you that I very much admire. And there are other bits that I don't. This keeping quiet is one of them. Ed, please, tell me.'

He stood quickly, walked over to look at Penny again. 'Better and better,' he muttered. 'Maddy, she's going to be fine.' Then, just as quickly, he came back to sit by her.

'We've got a minute,' he said. 'This will be hard for me—but I will tell you. I might regret it afterwards but I will tell you.'

Now Maddy was nervous. What was she going to hear?

'Penny Cox was double trouble,' he started. 'Because of the splenectomy she had an immunodeficiency problem and then she caught gastroenteritis. She could have died, but she's been very lucky. Some few years ago, in a hot and sweaty part of Africa, another Penny had exactly the same symptoms but with a further problem. She was four months pregnant. And she died. That was Penny Tremayne, my wife.'

Maddy winced. Never had she suspected his story could be as tragic as this. 'So this…brought it all back?'

'It did. We were in a desperate bit of Africa, I was running a bush hospital. There was an outbreak of gastroenteritis there and it spread like wildfire. The people there were mostly refugees from a neighbouring country and no one except us cared about them. They were malnourished, weak, they died like flies.' He pursed his lips, as if considering. 'But we did save some. We did some good.'

'Go on,' said Maddy.

'I had a tiny team of orderlies, not enough drugs, not enough helpers. This wasn't what I had joined the army for…but there were political considerations.'

Maddy found it hard to ask, but she had to. 'Was your wife in the army, too?'

'No. She was a nurse, working for an African charity. When she heard where I had been posted to she pulled a few strings and got leave to come to work with me. I didn't want her there, but she just turned up and refused to leave. How I wish I'd forced her back!' He paused and then said bitterly. 'But there weren't a lot of volunteers for the job.'

'She sounds a…fine woman, ' Maddy said carefully. 'You must have been proud of her.'

'It's wonderful being proud of a dead woman!'

For a moment there was raw emotion in his voice, and Maddy flinched. How could she ever have thought that this man was without feelings?

He went on, 'She had immunodeficiency problems from an earlier illness, she was pregnant, and I was working a twenty-hour day. Then she caught gastroenteritis. A day later we both knew she was dying. I sat by her bed, held her hand and wiped the sweat off her face.

We had so much planned together! Then an orderly came, saying there was a major problem that only I could solve. She knew this. She told me to go and get on with my job, there was nothing more I could do for her but I could save other people. So I left her—and perhaps I did save other people. But she died alone.'

He stopped a moment. Then, almost whispering now, 'I was leaving the army because my father had offered me a job. We were going to come back to Penhally, buy a house and settle down. I was so looking forward to being a father.'

That last sentence was the hardest thing to bear. Maddy knew there was nothing she could say. On impulse she wrapped her arms round him, rested her head against his chest. And, as she knew they would, the tears came.

He stroked her hair, the back of her neck. 'It's a long time ago,' he said. 'Don't be sad.'

He was comforting her!

So much made sense to Maddy now. 'That's why you weren't as pleased as Kate and I when the baby was born?'

'Possibly. But it would be mean-spirited to be envious of the parents' happiness.'

Maddy sighed, her heart aching for his pain. 'Ed, how you must have been suffering! All those memories flooding back. How could you bear it?'

'I was the best man for the job,' he said. 'But you're right. The memories have been…hard, especially seeing Penny here. It brought back all the agony, all the misery and the pointlessness of things, all the long waiting for life to seem better. And it never did. I was in love with my wife, I was enthralled with the idea of being a father and within twenty-four hours it all disappeared.'

His voice altered, became more curt. Now he was once again the professional, ex-military doctor, not used to talking about his emotions. 'I made a decision then. I never wanted to love like that again, because there was always the chance of loss. So I've avoided…emotional entanglements ever since.'

'Is that why you don't want to get too close to me?'

'It is. We agreed that this is just a shipboard fling and it doesn't count. I'm happy to be with you, Maddy, because I know it will end.'

'I see,' she said flatly.

He stood. 'You were right about one thing. It does help to tell someone else. But now that's over. Let's have a last check on Penny here and then we'd better get on our rounds again.'

So, back to business. There was work to be done, she had to concentrate on it. But she also had to think about Ed. Now she thought she understood him so much better. But did he have to be so certain about how he would live his life in the future?

It was a hard day but by the end of it things were obviously easing off. There were no new cases. More than a few people were still seriously ill but the medical team was coping.

Late that evening Ed called a meeting of all his little staff, thanked them for what they had done so far and said that he thought that things would be considerably better by the next day. The staff smiled. It felt good to know that you were on top of things. Ed went on to say that unless there were any objections they would stick to the same shift pattern. This would mean that he and Maddy would get to sleep for six hours again that night. Though either could be buzzed if there was an emergency.

Two hours later it was time for bed and Maddy met Ed outside her cabin. 'You look tired,' she said. 'It's getting to you at last.'

'No one can go on for ever.'

She looked at his unyielding face and said, 'I'm looking forward to my bed, but if you'd like a tea and whisky first, then I'll be making one.'

Rarely for him, he made a confession. 'I was so hoping you'd say that. But I thought it would be forward of me to ask.'

'I think we two are beyond being forward with each other,' she said tartly. 'Will you shower in your cabin or mine?'

'I'll shower in yours if I may. It makes it all seem a bit more…intimate.'

'It does indeed,' she agreed with a little smile.

So, shortly, they were sitting side by side in her bed again and tonight she hadn't bothered with her nightie. But she didn't feel like being too obvious. She tucked the sheet around her shoulders.

She looked at his face, trying to work out what he wanted from her. Simple sex? She didn't think so. If anything, she thought he needed companionship. It suddenly struck her that, in spite of being part of a large family, he might also be a lonely man. A man who seldom confided in anyone, who kept his feelings to himself. But he had revealed himself to her. The thought made her happy.

'Ed, what you told me in Penny's cabin. I'm glad I

know more about you. Sometimes you come across as being brilliantly professional—but there's always a reserve there. And I think I've got beyond that reserve.'

'There are things one needs to keep to oneself,' he said. 'Apart from anything else—why should I trouble other people with my problems?'

'Because they want you to trouble them,' she told him. 'Because they…I…think a lot of you.'

'Perhaps. Maddy, I think I…think a lot of you.'

'Good,' she said. 'And I think a lot of you, or we wouldn't be doing this.' A small part of her brain wondered if that was the most passionate declaration he was capable of. Still, she supposed it was something.

He smiled at her. Then he drew her to him and kissed her and she felt that whatever their problems, they could be solved. But now was not a time for problems in the future. Now was for now.

The night before their love-making had been at first tentative and then a desperate seeking for solace. It had been over quickly, because that had been what both of them had wanted—had needed. Tonight, even though they were more tired than ever, it was different. It was a gentler, more giving love-making. And she felt that it was love. He didn't use the word, but all his actions were those of a man who would do all that was possible for the woman he was with. They fitted together so well! They could both anticipate, knew what the other wanted, knew what would give most pleasure. And then there was a final climax that seemed to roll on and on for ever.

One final kiss and then it only was a moment before she could feel his chest rising and falling under her arm, hear the deep breaths of a man whose exhaustion had led him instantly to sleep. She felt exhausted, too.

Perhaps it was this fatigue that allowed an idea to surface, a thought that she had not permitted herself even to consider. Ed Tremayne. She admired his medical skill, she enjoyed being with him, sex with him was wonderful. But there was more than all that.

Now she knew she loved him.

She thought of what she had decided, or what had been revealed to her, and then slept at once. It was a deep sleep, but somehow the knowledge of the love was with her and it comforted her.

CHAPTER EIGHT

IT WAS a mistake, a big mistake.

Next morning was different from the morning before. This time she woke up first, checked the time. They had twenty more minutes together. For a moment she just lay there, looking at him. He was still asleep, and his face had that peaceful innocence that she had noticed before. It was the face of a new, different Ed. An Ed who had been hidden from her before. The lines drawn by pain had disappeared.

She remembered the night before, an almost startling realisation. Had it happened so suddenly? She loved him. More than that, she now felt capable of love again and that made her so happy.

She just couldn't resist. She knew he needed every minute of sleep he could get but... She leaned over him, just brushed his lips with hers. And his eyes flicked open immediately. She was so filled with happiness, filled with the realisation that her life had changed so much for the better, that she said it without thinking. It was so obvious to her.

'I love you, Ed.' It shocked her to hear herself say it. But, still, she waited for his reaction.

He had been asleep. But when he woke up he was alert at once. She saw him frown when he grasped what she had said. Why didn't he smile? Why didn't he say something?

He pushed himself up in bed, looked at her. 'What did you say, Maddy? I must be still asleep. I thought I heard you say you loved me.'

It was the wrong reaction, she thought. If you told someone you loved them, they should say it straight back. Or kiss you or something. Not ask foolish questions. Faltering, she said, 'Well, after last night… And it was so wonderful…I just thought that…' And then it hit her. They had made an agreement. This affair was to take place on board only—then it was to end. Yes, they liked each other, yes they had learned each other's secrets. But that had only been for a couple of snatched days.

She had made a terrible mistake. Shaking her head as if confused, she said, 'Sorry, I was just waking up. Not knowing what I was saying, dreaming really. Forget it.'

Even to herself this sounded lame but she managed to press on. 'Now it's time to get up. I'll go first in the shower and then we can…'

They were sitting side by side in her bed, he put his arm round her, pulled her towards him and kissed her on the cheek. On the cheek? This was a kiss you'd give your child or your grandmother. Not your lover.

His voice was kind, which made things worse. 'Maddy, you weren't dreaming. You said you loved me and you meant it. And I'm so sorry.' He shook his head in distress. 'I never intended this to happen. I knew what I was doing was wrong, I took advantage of you. When you're working in a stressed situation like we are, you do not start love affairs.'

This made her angry. 'No one took advantage of me. There were two of us involved—if anything, I made the first moves.'

'Then I should have resisted them.'

Silence for a moment. 'Thanks,' she said. 'That makes me feel great. Now, you stay in bed, I need the first shower.'

'But, Maddy, I…'

She slid out of bed, ran to her shower and locked the door. She turned the shower on full blast so the sound of it would hide her sobbing. And then anger took over and she stopped crying. She had made a fool of herself and she hated it.

From outside she heard the sound of a door clicking shut. He had got up and left her cabin. Well, she might as well carry on with getting ready for the new day.

When she left the bathroom, wrapped tightly in her dressing-gown, he had, of course, gone. Perhaps that was the best thing. Perhaps it would be best if she just forgot what she had said to him, just carried on as if nothing had happened. Shortly he would leave the ship and they would stick to their agreement—what they had was for on board the ship only.

But she knew she couldn't just forget Ed Tremayne. She did love him.

She had come on board this ship to be away from ma-rauding men. She had never wanted to think of love again. But she had found a man and she had fallen in love with him and he didn't want her. What to do?

She shrugged, smiled a bitter smile. There was nothing she could do but suffer.

She dressed, stayed in her cabin until she heard the sounds of the other staff coming into the medical centre. It was time for handover, the reports of staff who were coming off duty to those who were coming on. She'd be happier meeting Ed again if they were in company.

She went out, saw Ed talking to Dr Wyatt. 'Morning,' she said pleasantly. 'How are things going?'

She saw the faint relief in Ed's eyes, knew that he realised she was going to remain professional. Well, of course, she was going to remain professional. At the moment it was all she had going for her.

'Things are now definitely improving,' Ed reported. 'There are no new cases, the worst are improving, those who are nearly better are complaining about not being able to go on shore. I think we can congratulate ourselves.'

'In that case, may I have the morning to deal with the few patients who have problems other than gastroen-teritis?' Maddy asked him. 'There are some dressings to be checked and changed, some injections to be given. A few people I just like to keep an eye on.'

'Good idea. It's too easy to forget that there might be problems other than the gastro.'

She wondered if there were also the faint signs of relief in his voice at her suggestion. This way they wouldn't have to spend time together.

It was good to get back to her old job, good to be able to do it well. Apart from the medical attention she could spare the time to chat for a few minutes, instead of being in the vast hurry she'd been in recently.

Most of her patients were eager to get ashore now, some were quite annoyed. Maddy managed to calm most of them, making them feel relieved that they hadn't been infected themselves. It was all part of a cruise ship nurse's job.

But as the morning wore on she felt worse and worse. At first she thought that it was misery because of her mistake with Ed. Then she wondered if she was going down with the illness herself. That wouldn't be fair! She had been so careful with the necessary precautions. But then she decided that she was not showing any of the initial symptoms. She just felt dreadful.

Her last call was to Mrs Cowley's cabin. Robbie's dressing ought to be changed. Robbie's dressings got dirty faster than anyone else on the ship.

He wasn't in the cabin. 'His friend Joey just came to call,' Mrs Cowley explained. 'Came with his dad and asked if Robbie wanted to go to the play area with them. Well, he'd been getting restless and I felt a bit tired so I said he could go. They'll bring him back in time.'

'Feeling tired?' Maddy questioned. 'You are sticking to the diet, aren't you?'

'Well, sort of…'

For what must have been the tenth time Maddy went through the dangers of binge eating if you were diabetic.

Finally she left, telling Mrs Cowley that she'd find Robbie some time later. She still felt dreadful, so she decided to go back to the medical centre and have a drink of water. Was she dehydrated? She didn't think so. Perhaps it was just fatigue catching up on her.

Just as she thought this Ed came into the room. He looked at her and frowned. 'You don't look too good,

Maddy,' he said. His tone was medical, professional, but she thought she could detect some touch of personal feeling there.

'I'll be all right. It's catching up on me, I just need to sit down a moment.'

'We'd better make sure you're not coming down with the bug as well. Come into your cabin and I'll examine you.' There was a pause and then he said, 'Do you want a chaperone?'

She managed a small smile. 'I think it's a bit late for that now.'

They went into her cabin so he could examine her. She noticed that he took rubber gloves out of his bag—and then dropped them back in. 'You should wear gloves to examine every patient,' she told him.

'On this occasion I'll manage without.'

She knew why. The last time his hands had been on her body they had… To touch her again with rubber gloves would be an insult to them both.

He said, 'You know, Maddy, we have to talk and—'

She cut him off. 'Not now,' she said. 'I just can't deal with it. Perhaps not ever. Just get on with your work.'

It didn't take long and she knew what the result would be. 'Nothing too seriously wrong with you, Maddy. Nothing physical, that is. You've just done too much. A body can't take stress indefinitely. Now, pay attention to me. You're going to rest now. Just for three hours; I promise I won't leave you longer than that.'

'But, Ed, I'm needed.'

'Things are a lot better. You're not needed now.'

Telling her she wasn't needed was the wrong thing for

him to say, she saw that he recognised this at once. But he said nothing and neither did she. 'I'll do as you say,' she said.

The moment he had gone she remembered her last task—finding Robbie and re-dressing his arm. Well, it would only take a minute. She'd do that now and then have her rest.

First she went back to Mrs Cowley's cabin. No Robbie there. And Mrs Cowley was asleep. Having checked that she hadn't fallen into a diabetic coma, Maddy went up to the children's indoor play area. It was a large, glassed-in room with the usual games. There were ship attendants there and children being watched by their parents. The children's room was busy. The storm had abated slightly but it was still too cool and windy for anyone to go out on deck.

But no Robbie. Maddy said hello to a few people she knew, and asked about Robbie. Everyone knew Robbie. She was told he had been there playing with Joey Billings and his dad but he had left half an hour ago.

Maddy was now feeling slightly worried. But probably Robbie was in the Billingses' cabin. She went down to ask.

'Left the play area with us about half an hour ago,' Mr Billings said with a big smile. 'The boys had a great game of pirates. I took him down to his corridor, saw him walking to his cabin.'

'Did you take him into the cabin?'

Mr Billings looked uncomfortable. 'Well, no. I've been in there before… Often Mrs Cowley doesn't like to be disturbed.'

'So you didn't actually see him go into the cabin?'

'No. But he was only three doors away.'

Maddy thanked Mr Billings and left. Somewhere Robbie was wandering. There were an awful lot of attendants on the ship so he couldn't really get into mischief, could he? Possibly, yes. Robbie was gifted that way.

It would cause an awful lot of trouble and alarm to broadcast a request for people to look for a small boy in a pirate's outfit. She might have to in time, of course, but where could he be? Then Maddy remembered. Robbie wanted to be a pirate. And the pirate ship he wanted was one of the lifeboats—he'd been stopped from climbing on them before. He had pointed out to Maddy that if the cruise ship sank, this would be the best one for a pirate.

Maddy climbed to the lifeboat deck, and went out onto the deserted companionway. The wind wailed around her, pushing her back against the railings. There was absolutely no sign of Robbie. She walked closer to the lifeboats. From a distance they looked small but nearer they were quite alarmingly large. She spotted the one that Robbie wanted and went to stand underneath the lifeboat, looked up at the davits, the complex gear for swinging the boat out and lowering it into the sea. One last look around—no Robbie. She'd go back to the play area.

The biggest noise was still the wind but suddenly Maddy thought she heard something else. A cry, a whimper? But from where? Then she remembered that Robbie had had to be stopped from trying to climb on top of this lifeboat. Had he succeeded this time? 'Robbie,' she shouted, 'it's Nurse Maddy.'

'Nurse Maddy, help, I'm frightened,' a little voice came.

'Where are you?'

'I'm on top of the boat. And I'm slipping.'

Maddy looked up at the launching gear, saw how a determined little boy could have climbed up. Quickly she climbed onto the railings, reached up to where there was a handhold, a place to wedge her feet. Then somehow she wriggled upwards and came to where she could see the top of the lifeboat. There was a covering over it, two smooth sloping surfaces. And on one of the surfaces Robbie was stretched out. He had boarded his pirate ship. But there was nowhere to hang onto and he was in danger of slipping off the edge and falling. Possibly even bouncing into the sea. He knew it and he was terrified.

Somehow Maddy struggled a bit further upwards— Robbie must have been like a monkey to get up here with a bandaged arm! She mustn't alarm him, mustn't let him panic. 'How's the pirate chief, Robbie?'

'I want to get down!'

'All right. Now, you just stay there and I'll reach forward and grab your hands. Then I'll slide you towards me. But keep still till I reach you!'

Robbie nodded.

Maddy looked down. She was in a difficult position, her feet braced on a rail, one hand clutching a thick wire cable, the other hand stretching out to Robbie. Robbie grabbed for the outstretched hand, missed it and started to slip. Maddy lunged, just managing to get a hand to him, to grip him by the collar of his jacket. But with only one hand she didn't have the strength to pull him to safety. And now both she and Robbie were starting to slip. But she wouldn't let him go!

What to do now? It was something she had never done before. She cried out for help, hoping someone would hear her over the wind and sea.

Dimly she was aware of the rattle of feet on the deck below her. The strain on her arm was getting to be too much, she could feel her grasp on the cable loosening. She had to hang on!

CHAPTER NINE

ED'S morning had not been good. For once in his life he had absolutely no idea of what to do. And he didn't like being in doubt. It was driving him crazy.

He had just sent Maddy to bed—the bed he had climbed out of not four hours before—and walked away from the medical centre with his feelings in turmoil. Of course, he'd realised how hurt Maddy had been but as usual he'd managed—he thought—to hide his own feelings.

He thought back over the past two days. What decisions had he made and why? First, why was he on the ship at all? He knew his father could have dealt with the situation just as well as him. But he had insisted. This job had to be his.

The worst time of his life had been spent dealing with an epidemic, so why had he wanted to experience it again? In fact, he knew why. He had to face up to things, he couldn't go through his life knowing that he was afraid of something. And it had been hard but he had managed somehow.

Now he knew the crisis was almost over. He wasn't needed any more. He could go ashore knowing that he had done a good job And he had faced down his devils. Well, some of them.

But while the fear of the outbreak was behind him there was another, bigger problem. No, not a problem! Maddy was the best, the most exciting… No way could he call her a problem. But what should he do about her?

He had tried to be fair to her by telling her there could be no future in their affair. And later he had tried to explain why—how, after his wife had died, he'd never wanted to fall love again. Because of the risk of being hurt again. And this was unusual. He'd never felt the need to explain his actions to any other woman. So why Maddy?

And why had he felt some kind of peace or relief when he had told her? They had had a hard couple of days— probably it was good that the work had been so hard because so many memories, feelings had been dragged to the surface. The outbreak itself, the birth of a baby which had reminded him of his own unborn child. Penny, who had the same name and fatal combination as his dead wife—gastroenteritis and a compromised auto-immune system. But this Penny had survived and there had always been someone with her.

He had tried to insulate himself against these negative feelings. He couldn't, wouldn't suffer again.

He realised that he was going round in circles, not facing the big question. Could he give Maddy up? Always supposing she wanted to see more of him. Halfway along the corridor he made a decision and turned back to the medical centre. He had to see her. Never mind if she was tired, she must help him. He wasn't sure of what he was going to say to her, he just knew he had to say something.

Then he realised what he was trying to do. He was handing over responsibility to her. What did she think he ought to do? He had never done this before in his life. He was asking, not deciding. But he felt he had made some kind of a decision.

Back in the medical centre he tapped on Maddy's door then peered inside. No Maddy. A nurse came in to collect some more medicines, and when Ed asked her she said that she had seen Maddy two minutes ago on her way to the children's playroom. And she had looked terrible.

Ed nodded, rushing off to the playroom. There he was told that Maddy had just been in, asking for Robbie, and someone had seen her climbing up to the next deck. They didn't know what she was doing there. Ed wondered, too. There was nothing for her up there except lifeboats. Then it struck him. Robbie the devil who wanted to be a pirate. Who had already picked out the lifeboat he wanted as his pirate ship. Who had fallen off it once.

Ed ran up the stairs and out onto the lifeboat deck. It was windy, cold and there was no one about. No sign of Maddy or Robbie. He looked up and down and down and something flapping in the wind caught his eye. A scrap of blue—the colour of the scrubs Maddy was wearing. What was it doing halfway up a lifeboat davit? That was dangerous!

He ran along the deck, looking up to see Maddy precariously balanced, leaning over the lifeboat. She shouldn't climb in the state she was in! He shouted to her, then climbed up behind her, seeing her half-spreadeagled over the lifeboat canopy. She held Robbie by his jacket collar to stop him sliding off the edge of the canopy and into the sea. Her face was twisted with pain.

He was bigger, stronger, more fit than Maddy. He lunged forward, grabbed Robbie and dragged him under one arm. The three of them were balanced there. What should he do next?

'I'm all right for a minute,' Maddy gasped. 'I can hang on. You get Robbie down.'

He looked at her, thinking frantically. Was he abandoning another woman he loved? Then common sense took over. Carefully he climbed back down to the deck, keeping a tight arm round the little boy. For once, Robbie had the sense to stay still.

Robbie was now safe on deck, scared but otherwise fine. Ed looked up again to see the woman he now knew he loved.

Maddy's grasp loosened. He saw her plummet and desperately he dived to catch her but he just couldn't manage it. Her head hit the deck. And he recognized the sound that sickened him—Maddy had a fractured skull.

Feelings that he had hoped to forget rushed back so strongly that he had to choke back a cry of despair. This couldn't happen again! He loved Maddy!

It was nearly the hardest thing he had ever done. He was a doctor. Maddy was someone injured. What was needed now was professional skill, not emotion.

Calling to Robbie to stay where he was, he checked Maddy's vital signs. She was still alive. ABC—airway, breathing, circulation. All seemed, well, adequate. Still alive. The gentlest of palpations of the skull—yes, fractured. A delicate touch at the back of the neck. There appeared to be no damage to the spine but it was hard to tell.

He needed help! He buzzed the medical centre. Dr Wyatt

was there. 'I'm up on the lifeboat deck, starboard side. Come up yourself and get two stewards to bring up a stretcher. Maddy has a fractured skull. I want you here now!'

'On our way,' said Dr Wyatt. 'I'll bring some stuff and a hard collar.'

A distant bit of Ed's brain told him to remember to congratulate her on her quick thinking. He needed a hard collar and had forgotten to ask for one!

Now the captain. Ed buzzed again, told Ken, the captain's steward, to interrupt the captain, whatever he might be doing. This was an emergency. And while he waited for the captain to come on the line he looked at the sky. Yes, it looked possible.

'Yes, Dr Tremayne? Captain Smith here.'

It was good to hear that calm efficient voice. He would be calm, efficient himself. As much as he could. 'Captain, Maddy Granger has just had a bad fall and has a fractured skull. This is serious, far beyond my expertise. I'm taking her to the medical centre for now but she needs to go to hospital urgently. Is it possible now to get a helicopter to the ship?'

'I think so. I will see to it at once as a matter of extreme urgency. I'll ring down to the medical centre as soon as there is news.'

'The nearest competent hospital is St Piran's,' said Ed. 'The head of A & E is Ben Carter. I'll contact him.'

'Good. I'll arrange the helicopter transport.'

There was the rattle of feet on the deck and a horrified Dr Wyatt and two stewards ran up. Ed detailed one steward to take the now crying Robbie back to his mother. Then, with help, he slid Maddy's neck into the hard collar. Then they gently lifted their unconscious patient onto the stretcher and took her down to the medical centre.

Ed looked at her white face. Another white face kept flashing into his mind, and there was the memory of a death. Please, this couldn't happen again. But he had to concentrate!

In the medical centre Maddy was examined for other injuries. There didn't appear to be any. Just the skull. Just!

He looked down and his heart rate suddenly surged as Maddy's eyes fluttered open. She looked at him, blinked and waited for consciousness to arrive. 'Hello, Ed. I fell, didn't I? Is Robbie…?' and then she lapsed into unconsciousness again.

Twenty minutes later there was a phone call from Captain Smith. 'The chopper is on its way. Can you prepare to load the patient in half an hour?'

'I can.'

'How is she?'

'Holding her own,' Ed said. 'So far anyway. Captain, I want to go with her.'

'Of course. I think your work here is more or less done. Dr Wyatt can take over.' There was a tiny pause to show that the captain was moving from professional to personal and then he said, 'Ed, I want know what happens. Maddy—we all think a lot of her.'

'I'll keep you posted,' Ed promised. Then he turned to stare down at her.

Ten minutes after that there was another call, this time from his friend Ben Carter at St Piran's. 'You have a patient for me, Ed?'

For now this wasn't the woman he loved, this was a

patient. There was no time for emotion. 'She fell and smashed her head. Obviously she's concussed and she's drifting in and out of consciousness. Blood pressure up, slow pulse. I've taken X-rays, there's a depressed fracture and some fragmentation. I suspect a subdural haematoma, and I've got an IV line in to deal with any dehydration through blood loss.'

'Sounds like I need to see her urgently. I understand there's a chopper bringing her in?'

'That's right.'

'Well, I need to have a look at her and we need CT and MRI scans. Once I've got those we'll have her in Theatre. I'm getting the team together.' There was a short pause and then Ben said, 'Your voice is cracking, Ed. Is this girl a personal friend of yours?'

'I hope so,' Ed said quietly.

This was silly, Maddy thought. No, not silly, weird. She knew she was floating in and out of consciousness. The odd thing was, when she was conscious she was able to have quite intelligent conversations. Well, she thought they were intelligent. They just suddenly…stopped.

Her head hurt. But if she turned it slightly she could see an IV giving set dripping blood into her. Yes, she must have lost quite a lot of blood. That would be why she felt quite so weak and…

She knew that her injury was serious. Possibly extremely serious. She had seen it in the faces of Dr Wyatt and the nurses. Dr Wyatt had told her that this wasn't her area of expertise. She wondered what expert they might manage to find and if it would be in time. And where was Ed?

The odd thing was that this should have happened just when she was beginning to be able to feel again. Feel emotionally, that was. It was as if a black cloud had lifted. She could see possibilities all around her, saw that there were chances that she ought to take. Ought to have taken.

Ed Tremayne. She had started to feel something for him. Perhaps she should have fought harder against letting him go. Though where would that have got him now? More misery? She knew that this injury was serious. It would have been a pity if he had… She drifted off again.

Somehow she knew that quite some time had passed since she had last been conscious. And when she came to she knew that her condition had deteriorated. But she could still think clearly, even though it was an effort to open her eyes, to turn her head. And there was Ed. The man she loved!

He looked different. The old iron face had gone, she now could tell exactly what he felt. Of course, he was terribly worried. But there was something else that she wasn't quite certain of. A new expression on his face that she had never seen before.

He took her hand, lifted it to his lips and his eyes never left her face. 'You weren't here when I woke up before,' she said. She was amazed at how weak her voice sounded.

She thought he was fighting to keep his feelings under control. 'Did you think I wanted to leave you here to be injured on your own? It was so hard, leaving you! But there were things I had to arrange. We've got a helicopter coming to take you to hospital.'

'You're coming, too!' She didn't want to be parted from him.

'Of course I'm coming, too. You're going to see a friend of mine, Ben Carter. He's a surgeon.'

'So I need a surgeon? I'm that bad?'

'Ben had a look at your X-rays, we had a video connection. He wants to have a closer look.'

'You mean open up my head. So you know what's wrong with me?'

It was strange how weak she felt and yet how alert. Something to do with her injury? No, nothing like that. But she saw the doubt and fear in Ed's eyes and she guessed what he was not telling her.

'We're not sure yet. It'll all be clearer when Ben has operated.'

'Ed! The two of us have always been honest with each other. At least, we've tried, though I'm not sure how well we have succeeded. Now, never mind about reassuring the patient. Tell her honestly what her chances are.' She paused a moment to get her breath, and then went on, 'There are definite reasons I need to know.'

She saw him debating, wondering whether to tell her or not. She was glad when he decided to be honest.

'There is pressure from fragments of broken bone in your skull, causing bleeding into the brain. We don't know how serious the bleeding is, but it's got to be stopped soon. Ben needs to drill through to try to relieve the pressure, tie up the leaking blood vessels and deal with the bone fragments. He won't know how hard the job will be till he gets inside.'

'What are my chances?'

He didn't answer.

'Listen, Ed! I've been a theatre nurse in A and E, I know what skull fractures are like. I've seen enough road accidents. And you've turned into a terrible liar—you couldn't convince anyone. It's really important that I know the worst possible thing that could happen to me.'

He gave up trying to hide things from her, she was too certain about what she wanted. 'There's a risk that you could slip into a coma and never come out of it.'

She held his gaze. 'So what are the chances of that happening to me?'

He didn't answer at first. She could see his pain was even greater. But then she knew he would act like the doctor he was, the man who could do whatever was necessary, whatever it cost him. 'The chances of success are about fifty-fifty. Ben thinks that we daren't wait any longer. He's been talking on the radio to some expert in London, and the man agrees we need to operate at once. Your condition is deteriorating every minute.'

Strange how detached she felt, she thought. This was like talking about someone who wasn't her. 'That's more or less what I had guessed. Don't worry, I can take it.'

'You can take it! What about…?' Once again she saw the giant effort he had to make to calm himself. Then he went on, 'For the moment I'm your doctor. I have to ask you if you agree to this operation. You know the risks involved. I have to ask you if you are willing to sign the consent form.'

'I'll sign it now. Can you get it and fetch me a pen?'

She had a moment alone while he fetched the form. She considered, made a decision then wondered if it was the right one. 'Life's too short to spend changing my mind,' she muttered to herself. Life was too short? It could be even shorter now her decision was definite. But the prospect of the operation really didn't alarm her. It was something else.

Ed came back in the room held out a pen and paper. 'Read what it says,' he urged. 'I don't want you to…'

She scrawled her name across the bottom of the sheet. 'I'll read it afterwards,' she said. 'Just out of curiosity. Ed, sit down, there's something I want to say to you.'

He sat, took her hand again. 'Maddy, don't waste your strength. We can—'

'No. I need to talk. I have to because I might doze off again and that would be terrible. You said I had a fifty-fifty chance of pulling through. Well, in case I don't, there's something I want to say to you. If I might die, I think that I have licence to say it. I don't need to worry about whether it's proper or not. And, Ed, you don't need to say anything.'

She took a breath. Now she had decided, she had to hang on, just for a while longer. She could feel unconsciousness creeping up on her, but she had to say this first. 'Ed, I meant what I said this morning. I do love you. Forget all that rubbish about shipboard romance, about this being out of time, not to be thought about. I love you.'

Why that funny way he was looking at her? As if he'd just heard news that surprised him. As if something odd had just occurred to him.

He shook his head, as if not certain. Then he did jerk her into full consciousness. 'And I love you, Maddy,' he said. And, almost as if it was an afterthought, 'Will you marry me?'

But after that first wonderful shock she felt the clouds gathering in her head again. His face seemed to blur, she was sinking into something deep and warm and comforting. 'You certainly know how to make a girl feel good,' she managed to whisper. 'Now I've got something to dream about. Marry you? Of course I will.'

She knew she was smiling as she fell asleep.

For a moment Ed stared down at the unconscious Maddy. He'd just asked her to marry him and he knew that it was what he wanted. More than anything. He would marry Maddy and they would be happy together—if she survived. And suddenly fear hit him, stronger than ever. A fifty-fifty chance. How could he cope? He had lost one woman he loved—how could he bear to lose another?

Then he told himself not to be a coward. He had tried to avoid falling in love because of the pain that loss might bring. But now he knew that the risk was worth taking. He was in love. And it was wonderful.

'Not quite as bad as I had feared,' said Ben. 'X-rays are good but they don't tell the whole story. Can't be certain yet, of course, but I feel…reasonably hopeful.'

Ed supposed that this was the best that could really be expected from a surgeon. He watched as Ben stripped off his blood-spattered scrubs and threw them into a bin.

'They're bringing her to now,' Ben went on. 'You can go in if you like. She might just recognise you.'

Ed went into the recovery room. A nurse smiled at him and left them alone. Ed looked down at Maddy's pale face, half-hidden by a turban of bandages. There was a sudden surge of pity for something that wasn't really too important. When it wasn't fastened up for work, Maddy's hair was light brown, shoulder length, and he thought it beautiful. He suspected she was rather proud of it. But now much of it would have been cut away. It would take months to grow back. Well…things could have been much worse.

There were tubes in her arms and behind the trolley there were monitors giving a constant flow of information. Automatically he scanned them. No obvious cause for alarm. Things seemed to be fine.

He bent to kiss her cheek. He couldn't see much of her forehead. She didn't smell like the woman he had kissed so passionately the night before. Now there was the smell of antiseptic and that unforgettable theatre smell. No matter. It would pass.

He straightened, looked down at her. And her eyelids flickered. She saw him, her eyes opened fully. 'Hi, Ed,' she whispered. Then her eyes closed again.

'You made it,' he whispered. That was good enough.

CHAPTER TEN

THIS was a lovely room, Maddy thought. She had the room to herself and at the bottom of the bed she could see French windows that opened out to the garden, and beyond that the sea. In time she would be able to sit outside on the terrace and watch the boats sailing in and out of the harbour.

She wasn't really sure how things had worked out this way. As she had no family, no close relations, the captain had arranged with Ed for her to be transferred from St Piran's to this nursing-home in Penhally Bay. The company would pay for it. She had been asked if this was what she wanted. Maddy had been content to leave all the decisions, arrangements to Ed. He was good at this sort of thing.

That was…what was it?…three days ago. She had been sedated most of the time. She had seen Ed twice every day. But she hadn't been able talk to him, to make sense of what he was saying. She had just held his hand. But now she was recovering, she didn't have to sleep quite so much. And she could look about her. Think of the future.

She had been told that she was to expect a visit from

her doctor. Good. She was feeling more herself now, she was still weak, her head still hurt an awful lot, and when a nurse had brought her a mirror, she had thought that she looked terrible. How long before her hair would regrow? What kind of style could she try? Whatever, she thought having her hair half cut off might be bad—but things could have been so much worse.

Where was her doctor? She was waiting to see Ed.

She had thought about him and when she had been asleep she had dreamed about him. But she wasn't sure about him. She knew she was still weak, emotionally as well as physically, but soon she knew she would be her old confident self. Able to make her own decisions and to think about what had happened to her. Able to think about what she had said—and about what had been said to her. Everything might be different now. But she was looking forward to seeing Ed again.

A nurse came in, smiled and said, 'The doctor's coming to have a look at you now. Ready for him?'

Well, she was. Sort of.

But it was a definite disappointment when the doctor who came in was Nick. She couldn't stop herself. She said, 'I thought Ed was my doctor.'

Nick smiled at his patient. 'No. I told him that I would be the physician in charge. I'll tell you why in a minute. Ed can be a visitor, and I'm sure he'll be in to see you soon. And Ben Carter will be over to see you tomorrow—he'll want to admire his good work. Now, we'll have the medical examination first and then perhaps chat a while.' He turned to the nurse. 'Janice, could you remove…?'

It seemed odd to be examined instead of examining. It

was weird to have your records looked at, instead of looking at them. She wasn't sure she liked it. But Nick was a professional. If nothing else she could admire his skill.

Finally the examination was over, her head was bandaged again and Nick told the nurse she could go. Maddy looked at him thoughtfully. He seemed to have relaxed. Now he was her friend. 'So why not Ed as my doctor?' she asked him. 'I thought he was very efficient.'

'He is efficient and I'm proud of him and his ability. But he's better not being your doctor because he can't keep the necessary distance. Because of the relationship between you two.'

'I'm not sure there is one,' she said. 'Things said in…in emotional moments aren't always true when you think about them dispassionately. You get over-eager.' Then, wanting some kind of encouragement, she asked cautiously, 'But if there was any kind of relationship, would you approve?'

'It's not my place to say. But I do find you a very competent nurse.'

Maddy felt just a little irritated. 'Thanks for the compliment—I think. Nick, are you always so guarded about what you say? It must be hard when so many of your patients are known to you. Are your friends, in fact.'

She was a bit surprised at the strength of his answer. 'Of course I'm guarded. Doctors aren't like most people, Maddy, you should know that. You have to keep some distance, if only because you learn so many secrets. Now, let's move onto something else. You can't go home alone so you're to stay here until we think you're fit to be discharged, and that'll be a while. You don't recover from cranial surgery quickly. So what do you see as your future?'

'I just haven't thought about it,' she said honestly. 'I suppose I could get another job with the cruise line. But I only signed on for one trip.'

'After your operation that won't be a good idea for several months. You need to be on dry land, within easy distance of a hospital. Not that I see any trouble ahead. But it's good to be cautious.'

He paused a moment, then said. 'I've been very impressed by you, Maddy. And when you worked for me before, you were excellent. Would you like to think about a job in the Penhally Bay practice?'

She looked at him in amazement. The thought had never crossed her mind. 'Is there a vacancy?'

'There will be shortly. We're expanding rapidly.'

She thought some more. 'Did Ed put you up to this?'

'No, it was entirely my idea. And I didn't ask him. I'm always on the lookout for good staff. Don't answer now, just think about it.'

He stood, picked up his doctor's bag. 'Ed's working this morning but he said he'd be in to see you this afternoon. You might like to talk about my offer to him. Bye, Maddy.' Then he smiled, taking her hand. 'It's good to see you looking so well. When I heard about your accident, I was worried.' And he was gone.

Maddy lay back on her pillow, wondered if the thinking she now had to do might make her head hurt even more. The offer of a job in the Penhally Bay practice. Working with Ed. Suddenly life seemed more complicated. Or more simple?

When she had only known Ed for three days she had told him that she loved him. Well, perhaps she hadn't been in her right mind, she had been about to have a possibly life-threatening operation. The trouble was, now she had had her operation, now she had been told that she was going to recover, she still knew that she loved him. And she had decided that she loved him before her accident. All right, sane, professional, reasonable nurses didn't make that kind of decision after three days. But she had. And she meant it.

She had told Ed that she loved him and he had promptly asked her to marry him. But had he only done it to aid her recovery, to make her feel better? In that he had been successful. She was sure that the proposal had helped her pull through. But had he really meant it? Had it just been the agony of the moment, a sudden rash decision to be later regretted? He wasn't ready for the consequences. And he was still upset over his dead wife, he just wasn't capable of making big decisions. Not for the rest of his life, it seemed to her. She was thinking clearly now, it was all so plain. He hadn't really meant it. No way could she hold him to a promise made so quickly.

What to do now? Ed was an honourable man. He had asked her to marry him. She thought she had said yes but she wasn't really sure. So he would want to do the proper thing—marry her. She must tell him that agreeing to marry him had been a mistake.

So the decision was made and the tears flowed again. But when they had passed she found herself stronger, determined. She knew what she had to do.

He came into her room that afternoon. It was a warm day, he was dressed in fawn chinos and a dark blue, open-necked, linen shirt. The blue of the shirt contrasted with his tanned face and he looked absolutely gorgeous. In one hand he had a bunch of flowers, in the other hand a silver-wrapped box that she guessed would hold chocolates. She didn't think she'd ever seen a more wonderful sight come into a patient's room.

He laid the flowers and the parcel on her bedside table, kissed her on the cheek, took her two hands and sat on her bed. 'So how are you?' he asked. 'You look so much better than when I last looked at you. It's good to see you improving.'

'I'm fine. I'm still weak but I'm getting better by the minute. And it's good to see you, too, Ed.'

'Know what day it is? It's Tuesday. Exactly a week since we first met.'

A week? Was that all? Half her life seemed to have been crammed into those few days. 'It seems longer,' she said. 'But only a week? We hardly know each other.'

'We've known each other since the moment we met.'

'No, we haven't. You were decidedly cautious with me when we first met. And I was cautious with you, felt that I'd met men like you before.'

'We got over that caution quite quickly. I kissed you. And you kissed me back.'

He didn't need to remind her. She remembered so well!

'But we were busy most of the time. What time did we have to get to know each other?'

'Two wonderful nights in a small bed,' he told her. 'Remember those?'

She did remember. How well she remembered. 'I'd blush if I could,' she said. Then, because she had to be honest, she said, 'I don't think I'll ever forget them.'

'Nor me.' He looked at her cautiously. 'What do you remember about what we said after you'd fallen and cracked your skull?'

She had to be careful here. 'I was confused,' she said. 'I just remember talking to you. You were comforting but I can't remember quite how.'

'I was comforting. In fact, you told me that I knew how to make a girl feel good. That pleased me.' He was looking at her with a half-smile on his face. 'It's not like you to be coy, Maddy. One of thing things I love about you is that you're direct and honest. So tell me, how did I make you feel good?'

No way could she lie, pretend she couldn't remember. Apart from anything else, it was a memory she wanted to cherish. 'You asked me to marry you,' she mumbled.

'I did.' He leaned over and kissed her again. 'One of the best things I've ever done in my life. And then you said that you would marry me. Proposal and acceptance. We're an engaged couple.'

From his pocket he took a tiny leather box, held it out to her. 'Open it. It's for you. Just until we can decide upon something better.'

The excited half of her desperately wanted to open the box, the wary half knew that it wasn't a good idea. The excited half won. Inside the box was a cushion of red silk and set into the cushion was a ring. It was worn with long use, but the stones—a pattern of emerald and jade—were as bright as ever. 'It's lovely,' she cried.

'It was my great-grandmother's engagement ring. This morning I asked my father if I could have it and he said yes.'

'Did he know you wanted it for me?'

'Well, I haven't been seeing any other woman recently,' Ed said mildly. 'I think he must have guessed.'

Maddy started to take the ring out of the box and then thrust it back. She knew that if she tried the ring on then she would never want to take it off. She gave the box back to Ed. 'You don't like it?' he asked in some surprise. 'Well, no matter. We can—'

'Ed! We've got to talk. It's so lovely but I can't take this ring. We just can't get engaged. I know you asked me to marry you and I said yes, but we were both over-emotional. We weren't thinking right. Things are different now.'

He looked surprised. 'Some things are different. I'm now not terrified that you might never come to after the operation. But the important things are still the same. I love you. And you love me—don't you?'

There was no way she could bring herself to say that she didn't love him. But she didn't have to answer the question directly. 'We were both tired, both emotional. I'm not going to take advantage of something you said when you weren't…when you weren't…'

'I think you're entitled to because I took advantage of you,' he said, with a grin that almost made her melt. 'I knew you were emotional and tired—but I still got into bed with you. Maddy, no way are you taking advantage of me. Don't you think that I don't know what I want?'

It was a hard thing to do but she felt she had to hurt him—even if it mean hurting herself more. 'Ed! You're still in love with your wife! You think of her all the time!'

She didn't get the reaction she had expected. He looked thoughtful rather than hurt or angry. 'I loved Penny,' he said after a while. 'I always will. But she's gone now and I can accept it. I've mourned her but now I'm over it. You helped me get over it. And, Maddy, I know she'd not have wanted me to spend the rest of my life just clinging onto a memory.' Almost as an afterthought he added, 'I also know she'd have liked you.'

That was such praise. For a moment Maddy was overwhelmed, didn't know what to say. One last argument. 'You also told me once that you'd felt such pain when your wife died you never wanted to risk it again.'

'How do you think I felt when I saw you go into Ben's operating theatre? I discovered then that any pain is worthwhile for someone you love. And I love you, Maddy. Being apart from you would hurt me so much.'

She could think of no further arguments. Gently, she lowered her head onto the pillow, stared at the flowers he had brought her. They were beautiful. What should she say now?

'You're tired.' His voice was tender. 'And you've been ill. It's wrong of me to push you. You need to sleep. I'll leave you now.'

He leaned over her, his lips brushed hers. 'Shall I leave this ring with you? Just so you can think about it?'

'Better not. It's too beautiful. The temptation to put it on might be too great, and then I'd never want to take it off.' She decided to make one last appeal. 'Ed, why don't we not talk about it for a year? Just carry on as friends. You can ask me to marry you in a year's time, when we've got to know each other better, when I'm fully well.'

'I don't want to wait a year. I love you now. And you love me, don't you?'

She couldn't bring herself to lie. 'Yes, I do love you and that's why I won't marry you. Not yet anyway. '

He sighed. 'Right, then. Maddy, I'm not allowed to bully helpless patients, it's against the doctors' code. But don't think I won't ask again! Now, I can't come to see you tomorrow, I'm going to London on a week's course. It was arranged months ago. But could I ring you tomorrow night?'

She reached for his hand, took it to her lips and kissed it. 'I'll be sad if you don't ring,' she said.

Ed drove up onto the moors. He didn't know how to deal with the turbulence of his feelings. Over the past week he had suffered a greater excess of emotions than at any time since—well, at any time since his wife had died. He realised that since then he had been coasting along, only half living. He had deliberately cut himself off from feelings—doing his job, taking a mild pleasure in the sea and countryside, occasionally taking out a girl who knew right from the beginning that it was nothing serious. Now none of that was good enough. He had started to feel again. And discovered that feelings could bring great joy.

He had promised to drop in at the Clintons' farm, to see how Isaac was getting on. Once again he was met at the farmhouse front door by Ellie. But this time she was in working clothes, boots, jeans and a decidedly scruffy-looking T-shirt. But he thought she looked well. There was a smile on her lips, a sparkle in her eyes.

'Dr Tremayne, how are you? The gossip is that you've been saving lives out on a cruise ship.'

'All part of the day's work, Ellie. Tell me, how was the St Piran's Ball?'

'It was wonderful! Do you know a Dr Peter Hunter who works there? He's a junior registrar in the ortho-paedic department.'

'Don't think I know him,' Ed said cautiously. 'You met him there?'

'I spent most of the night dancing with him. Oh, and other people as well. But…he's driven over to see me a couple of evenings.'

'Be careful of forming a relationship with a junior registrar,' Ed warned her. 'They work even longer hours than farmers.'

Ellie laughed. 'Early days yet. But I'm glad I went. Come inside, I'll get you a drink. You've come to see Dad?'

'Just a casual visit,' Ed said, skating around the truth. 'I was in the area and I thought I'd drop in.'

'He'll be pleased to see you but there's no real need. Since you talked to him last week he's been perfect. Done everything you told him to. He grumbles, of course, but he wouldn't be my father if he didn't.'

'Sounds like one of my successes,' said Ed.

In fact, he didn't really need to examine Isaac. The old man was obviously looking after himself and was feeling much better for it. Ed spent a quarter of an hour chatting to him and then set off for home.

He thought about Ellie as he drove down into Penhally. About how happy she seemed to be with her new doctor friend. Why couldn't he be as happy as that? He realised what he had lost or would lose if he couldn't marry Maddy.

He loved her. He thought she loved him—but she had this idea in her mind that they had to wait. He didn't want to wait. So…

He had a military mind so he would consider this a battle. The first thing you did when fighting a battle was look for allies. Allies! Now he had a plan.

CHAPTER ELEVEN

MADDY had no clear memory of Ben Carter. She knew he had operated on her, had been there when she had come round, but that was all. Now she met him properly. A tall, lean, smiling man with brilliant blue eyes. Were all the men in Penhally Bay gorgeous?

'Basically I'm a general surgeon, not a brain man,' he told her as he examined her next morning. 'Done a bit of skull work, of course, wondered about specialising in it at one time. But mostly it's general. Good thing you were out of it when I came to see you. You might have objected otherwise.'

'Ed seemed to think you were the best there was.'

'The best there was available. He was in a hurry—which incidentally was necessary.' He smiled. 'By the way, did you know you were operated on by television?'

'What? Television how?'

'I was linked up with a surgeon in London. I had a headset on while I was operating with a camera showing what I was doing. He offered advice.'

'I've heard of that kind of thing.'

'Set up by your friend and mine, Dr Ed Tremayne. He thought it might be a good idea. You know, the ex-military mind can be very impressive. Possibly you owe your life to Ed. He decided what needed doing, organised it at once and then saw it through. I wasn't the obvious choice to operate on a skull but I was the nearest, the most available. And time was running out for you. So he decided, coolly, logically, just like a machine. But he can feel, too. I've never seen him look so desperate. I had to send him out of the room while I operated. Are you two close?'

'Sort of,' Maddy said.

'He's a friend of mine but he's a good man,' said Ben. 'And he deserves a good woman.'

The nurse had unwrapped the bandages round her head and Maddy could feel the cool air on bare skin where there shouldn't be bare skin. She must look a mess!

Ben seemed to guess what she was thinking. 'We had to shave some of your hair off,' he said. 'But you know it'll grow back. You'll be as beautiful as ever. And though I say it myself, I did a pretty good job. You're going to make a complete recovery, Maddy.'

Ben stepped back while the nurse began to put fresh dressings on Maddy's head and started to write up her notes.

'Take things easy for a while,' he said. 'Nick Tremayne will keep an eye on you and I'll be back in a few days just to check up that all is well. But you can get up for a while…say tomorrow. Nothing too energetic. Just a short trip outside. Remember, Maddy, you were lucky. Be glad that you had Ed Tremayne on your side.' And he was gone.

Maddy lay back on her pillows and considered. Two things that she had not quite thought about yet. One, she possibly owed her life to Ed. Two, he had been desperate when he'd seen how ill she had been. She was not sure what to make of the two facts. But she thought about them.

An hour later she had another visitor. 'Hi, fellow midwife,' a voice called out, and there was Kate Althorp. She came over, kissed Maddy on the cheek. 'Can't say I care for the new-style headdress.'

Maddy smiled. She liked Kate, she was uncomplicated. The two of them had got on well when they had worked together on the ship. They had bonded as a team. She had hoped to see her again.

'I would have come to see you sooner,' Kate explained. 'But a mum-to-be came in with antepartum haemorrhage, Nick and I looked at her and diagnosed placenta praevia. But we got there in time. With any luck she'll go full term and the baby should be okay.'

She pulled a letter out of her pocket. 'And I wanted to see you anyway. I've got something to show you, something we did together.' She handed Maddy the letter.

There were two pictures of a baby—tiny but perfect. And a letter from Sarah Flynn. Quickly Maddy read it. Sarah apologised for sneaking onto the boat while she had been pregnant, said that baby Marina was now fine and thriving and that it was due entirely to Maddy and Kate. Many thanks. And she was writing to the chairman of the cruise line to congratulate him on the quality of his nursing staff.

'Nice to be thanked, isn't it?' Kate said. 'It's one of the reasons I took up midwifery. You usually get a happy result.'

'You're a local midwife and this is quite a small town,' Maddy said. 'You must see a lot of the children you brought into the world.'

Kate grinned. 'I do. And sometimes I regret having done so.' Her eyes twinkled. 'Now, what I thought was—'

The door opened, and there was Nick Tremayne. He looked from Maddy to Kate, obviously surprised. 'Kate? What are you doing here?'

'Maddy and I were midwives together, remember? I called in to say hello.'

Maddy saw an exchange of glances between the two, wondered if there was some hidden message that was not for her to know. Then she decided she was imagining things.

'I've just had a word with Ben,' Nick said. 'He's happy with your progress and suggests that you might like to get out of bed, perhaps tomorrow. I'm happy with that.'

'I was going to offer to take Maddy for a ride,' said Kate. 'She needs some fresh air.'

'As long as she takes it easy.' Nick turned and left.

For a moment Kate stared at the door through which Nick had left and Maddy was puzzled the odd expression she saw on Kate's face. 'I know the two of you work at the same practice,' she said. 'I mentioned before, you seem to be more than just close friends.'

Kate shrugged. 'We've known each other for years. In fact, we were teenagers together and…quite close. But then we went our different ways. Both of us married and both of us were happy. And then his wife died and my husband was killed.'

'Ed's wife died, too,' Maddy said. 'And none of you re-married. Is there anything between you and Nick?'

Kate tried to laugh. 'There's nothing between us,' she said. 'We are friends and we do work together. Anyway, he can be a grumpy old so-and-so when he wants to be.'

Maddy realised that this wasn't something Kate wanted to talk about. Then she forgot her interest when she heard what Kate had to say next.

'I had a phone call quite early this morning from Ed,' Kate said. 'He didn't want to disturb you but the message is for you. He'll phone tonight but he wanted you to know this at once. About a Brian something who you once knew.'

'Brian Temple. I knew him all right.' Maddy had forgotten telling Ed about Brian. Now his name brought out new worries. Brian would find it easy to discover what had happened to her, easy to discover where she was. He would come here, she knew it! And then... 'What did Ed say?' she asked in a panic.

Kate put a reassuring hand on her shoulder. 'There's no cause for alarm, Maddy. Ed said that you weren't to worry, it was all under control. He's been in touch with an army psychologist and Brian was offered treatment, which he's accepted. Ed says that all will be well.'

'Just like that? That man spoiled my life for months.'

Kate smiled. 'The Tremayne family tends to get things done.'

It was good to be among friends, Maddy thought. And she knew she could confide in Kate. 'I thought I was in love with Brian,' she muttered. 'He was a very determined man, ex-army like Ed. He got things done too, and at first I liked him for it. But then he came back from some mission with PTSD—post traumatic stress disorder—and there was just no living with him. I thought he'd turned into a monster, then I realised he'd always been one. He was madly jealous of everything I did, every friend I had.

There was no end of mental abuse, and I knew in time that it would turn physical. So I left him and he stalked me and made my life a misery. So much for love.'

'Love is wonderful,' Kate said after a while, 'if you get it right. But getting it right isn't easy. Now, Nick's signed your pass so would you like to come out for a ride for a couple of hours tomorrow?'

'I'd love to,' said Maddy.

There had been a lot of excitement during the morning. In the afternoon Maddy was taken out onto her terrace, put in the shade and told to rest. She decided that she was getting better. So that meant she couldn't be an invalid much longer, she had to start thinking about her future. Then she decided, not yet. She couldn't put up with it yet. There was too much to worry about.

That evening the telephone trolley was wheeled to her bedside, she was told that there would soon be a call for her and she was left on her own. When the phone rang she had to stop herself from grabbing for it. No need for Ed to think she was desperate for a call.

'Hi, sweetheart, how are you?' It was Ed. And her heart bounded.

'Hi, Ed. I'm fine. I'm improving. I've had visitors— Ben Carter, Kate Althorp and your dad.'

As so often there was a smile in his voice. 'Living the social round without me. It's all happening in Penhally Bay.'

'So how was your day?' she asked.

'Long but interesting. There's a new treatment for diabetes. It looks good and I'll try to persuade the practice to try it out.'

It was good to sit and chat to him. But suddenly she wanted him by her, she wanted his physical presence. Just so she could see him, hold him if she wished. 'Tell me where you are,' she said rather sadly.

'I'm in my hotel room. I should be looking through my notes, but…don't laugh. I'm reading *Pride and Prejudice*.'

Maddy couldn't help a little giggle. 'You!'

'Yes. And I've just got to the bit where Darcy has apparently given up the idea of marrying Elizabeth. But I've not given up. I still want to marry you right now. But I know you're ill so I won't push you.'

'Ed, for the good of both of us, forget it for a while. I may be ill but I'm not mad. Let's wait for a year and see how we feel then.'

His voice was serious. 'It's how I feel now that's important. How we feel. I love you, Maddy.'

'I love you, too,' she said. 'But I'm not going to change my mind about marrying you.'

It was sunny again next day. Well, she was entitled to a few sunny days after the storm the week before. In the afternoon a nurse helped her dress. It seemed strange to be putting on clothes that she hadn't seen for so long. Her clothes? How had they got there?

'Dr Tremayne organised it all,' said Samantha, the nurse who was dressing her. 'Dr Ed Tremayne. He got a lady doctor on the ship to pack for you.'

Organisation. She might have guessed.

It wasn't what she wanted but she was taken in a wheelchair to the front door, where Kate was waiting for her in her car. 'My hours tend to be irregular,' Kate said. 'Babies arrive to suit themselves. So I can often take time off when I need to. We'll take a couple of hours and you can look around Penhally Bay and the countryside.'

They went up onto the moors first, saw the great sweep of green, the blue of the sea beyond. Maddy felt that it was wonderful to breathe fresh air again, something different from the all-pervasive hospital smell she was so used to. Then they drove into the little town and she was shown the harbour, the walk along the beach. Then up to the surgery. It was a beautiful white building.

'We could go inside and have a look around,' Kate suggested. 'Who knows? You might find yourself working there.'

'Why do you say that? Has Nick said anything to you?'

'No. He keeps his ideas to himself a lot of the time.' Kate shrugged. 'But we are expanding, Nick is always on the lookout for good staff and I know he thinks well of you. Anyway, what are you going to do when you've recovered? Off on a cruise ship again?'

'I just don't know! At the moment my life seems all over the place.'

There must have been stress in her voice, because Kate patted her hand comfortingly. 'Don't worry about it. You've still not recovered. But all will come out well in the end.'

They drove on, came up to the church and saw a line of cars outside. But there were only one or two people about. Kate pulled up where they could have a good view of the church gate. 'I love a good wedding,' she said. 'The bride must be just about to arrive. Let's watch.'

Maddy was quite happy to sit and watch. They saw a

vintage, open-topped car draw up, two bridesmaids help the bride out of the car, smooth down her dress and adjust her veil.

'She looks good in plain white,' Kate said in a judicious voice, 'it suits her colouring. Would you get married in pure white, Maddy?'

Maddy shook her head. She was rather enjoying herself. She hadn't had a girly conversation about clothes in months. 'Pure white makes me look washed-out. I'd go for ivory. What's that material? I like it.'

'It's raw silk. Creases easily but hangs beautifully.'

They watched as the bride took the arm of her father and walked towards the church. Dimly heard organ music swell to greet her.

'I know the girl,' Kate said. 'Rowenna Pennick. Her father's a fisherman. She met a visitor last summer, a solicitor from London, and now she's marrying him.'

'And going back to London to live?'

'No. He's found a job down here. It's surprising how often that happens.'

They drove on, slowed as they passed another handsome stone building. 'That's Nick's house,' Kate said.

Maddy wondered at her flat tone. 'It's lovely. Does he live there all on his own?'

'Yes he does now. Whether anyone else will ever move in, I just don't know. Now. See what we have here. One bit of the family hasn't moved very far.'

They pulled up outside a whitewashed cottage and Maddy fell in love with it at once. 'Whose is it?' she asked, although she already had a good idea.

'It's Ed's cottage. Like to look inside?'

'But we can't. He's in London somewhere.'

'He always leaves a spare key in the surgery. I phoned him last night. There are some notes I need to see and he has them in his desk. I'm going to pick them up. Come and have a look.'

Maddy so much wanted to. She thought that you could tell a lot about a person by their home and she wanted to know more about Ed. Just out of curiosity, of course. 'Won't he mind?' she asked.

'Not at all. If I can go in, then you can, too.'

'Maybe just the front room,' Maddy said. In fact, she wanted to see the whole house, spend a couple of hours dreaming there. But the front room would do.

Kate helped her out of the car and she walked cautiously to the front door—through a tiny hall and then into the front room.

'Sit down,' said Kate. 'It'll take me a minute to run through these papers.'

So Maddy sat and looked about her. The room was even more lovely than the outside suggested. A through room, with the front facing the road and French windows at the back, overlooking a tiny patio and then the sea. It had a black wood-burning stove set into an alcove.

The room itself was fine, but…it needed something.

'He hasn't been here long,' Kate said, noting Maddy's interest. 'He hasn't really moved in, has he? It's all a bit bare.'

'Did he buy the curtains and the carpet?' Maddy asked. 'Did he decide on wallpaper rather than paint?'

Kate chuckled. 'Who's a little nest-builder, then?' she asked. 'You're right—wallpaper, curtains and carpet all came with the cottage. They need replacing. What this place needs is a woman's touch. Now, I've found my papers. We'd better get you back.'

Maddy had really enjoyed her outing with Kate. It had left her pleasantly tired—but in some ways strengthened. Now she could think. Decide on things.

She loved what she had seen of the moors, of Penhally Bay. She could be happy here. She had loved Ed's cottage and there was so much she could do to it. Kate was right, it needed a woman's touch. New carpet and curtains, redecoration. The furniture was fine but the room needed vases with flowers in them, pictures, photographs. She wondered what the kitchen, the bathroom were like. The bedroom…

This was silly! She was daydreaming when she ought to be making decisions about her future. What was she to do?

She had accepted it, she loved Ed. She had lost all her old fears. Ed could be the man for her, she would be happy with him. And she knew he loved her. Or he thought he loved her. That was the problem. Would he be happy with her?

The trouble with Ed was his sense of honour, his determination to do whatever was right. His dying, pregnant wife had told him to leave her side to help those he could save. And he had done it. He'd listened to her. And had suffered for it ever since.

She couldn't allow him to make another mistake. To discover after a few months that the woman he had married was not the one he needed. He was in too much of a hurry. He had to have time, whether he knew it or not.

Could she give him time? One thing was certain—she couldn't live here with him, just waiting. She'd have to get on with her life to give him time to get over her—if he wanted to.

So, she had made her decision. She knew it was the right one. And she hated it.

Samantha came back into the room. Maddy asked her if there was a copy of the *Nursing Times* she could borrow. Time to look for a new job. Did she want to go back on a cruise ship? No. She had enjoyed it but she knew it would never be the same again. A large city A and E department? Possibly. But after looking around Penhally Bay, large cities had lost their attractions. But she had to carry on looking.

That night the trolley was wheeled to her bedside again, and Ed phoned almost at once. He asked after her, was pleased she had gone out with Kate. Maddy didn't tell him that she had been in his home. He might ask what she thought of it, how it could be improved, and she didn't want to go into that.

He was good company, even on the phone. He told her a story about one of the delegates falling asleep and snoring during a lecture. The lecturer had said that he could accept a subtle hint that he had gone on for long enough. She loved listening to him, talking to him.

But there were things that she had to say. 'Ed, I'll tell you now so as not to hurt you. Your dad offered me a job and I would love it. But I've decided definitely to leave Penhally Bay. We need to be apart for a while.'

His voice was gentle. 'Maddy, I want to marry you. I feel that way now and I'll feel that way in a year's time and in fifty years' time. But not if you're unsure. So just don't decide anything yet. I'll be back soon and I'm so much looking forward to seeing you.'

There were plenty of tears when she rang off.

Next morning there was a message that Kate was coming to take her out again. Good. Maddy felt that she needed to be with a friend. After a while, even the best of nursing-homes got a little claustrophobic. And she could gossip about the Tremayne family, though it was a bitter-sweet experience. Not just Ed, of course. All the Tremayne family.

She managed to dress herself but with a nurse hovering near, in case she was needed. Then she insisted on walking to the front to meet Kate—but once again with a nurse in attendance. It would be great when she could look after herself again!

Kate was waiting, kissed her on the cheek again. 'You look better every day,' she said. 'Now, we'll try something a bit more exciting today. We're going to meet Angie, an old friend of mine. She's a dressmaker, just set up in business but doing very well for herself. It's your birthday soon, isn't it?'

Maddy was surprised. 'Yes, it is. But how did you know that?'

'There was a phone call to the practice from your Captain Smith. The cruise line and he want to give you a birthday present. Something a little bit different, a bit special. They asked my advice—I said an evening dress. It always cheers a woman up.'

'But I never get the chance to go out in evening dress!'

'The odd thing is, once you get the gown then opportunities to wear it mysteriously appear. So let's go and see what Angie can do for you.'

They drove across the moors again. Maddy wasn't really interested in a new evening dress. She looked a mess, her head was half-shaved and covered in bandages. She couldn't wear an evening dress looking like this. But Kate's enthusiasm was infectious and so she decided she'd enjoy the trip out.

Angie was tall, thin, serious and dedicated. She worked from the ground floor of a large house. There were lots of fabric samples on view, patterns and pictures on the wall. She looked at Kate with a critical eye and said, 'You've got the perfect figure for a long dress. Just enough fullness, enough curves in the right places.'

'Thank you,' said Maddy, wondering if she'd been complimented.

'Have you any style in mind?'

Maddy hadn't. 'I'm not sure,' she said. Then, not wanting to disappoint anyone, she said, 'I'm not quite myself, you know. But in general I like flowing lines and an absolute minimum of decoration. And not too low-cut.'

'Hint but not state,' Angie said approvingly. 'Look at these patterns here.'

It was fun, the three of them looking through the patterns. But eventually Maddy decided on one, and the other two agreed that it would be a perfect choice. It was simple but elegant. Maddy's mood changed a little. She wanted to wear this dress.

'Now fabric and colour,' said Angie. 'I've got some swatches here.' She looked at Maddy's face with the same considering expression and said, 'You've an autumn colouring. Look at these shades, warm with a touch of darkness.'

Maddy looked. And eventually she decided on a heavy

bronze silk-linen mixture. Because it was a mixture there was a subtle change in colour as she moved. It matched her hazel eyes beautifully and would go well with her hair. When her hair was on show.

She thought there had been times in the past when she would have loved this. But now wasn't the time. It would be nice to have the dress, but when could she wear it? Who would be her partner?

Now she had to stand in the middle of the floor with her arms outstretched as Angie took her measurements. It didn't take long. Then Angie stood back with a satisfied expression and said, 'That's all I need for now. And I gather this is to be an express job? I'll have it ready for fitting in a couple of days.'

Maddy looked at her in bewilderment. 'That fast? It usually takes weeks.'

'Only if you hang about,' said Angie.

Maddy was getting better, and every day now she felt stronger. Ed phoned each night and they chatted about what he had done, how she was feeling. But he never asked her about her future plans and she never told him. He didn't mention marriage again, and she didn't bring up the subject either. Perhaps he had given up the idea completely. Had decided to accept what she said?

That thought made her feel strangely unsettled.

After two days she was called for by Kate and taken to Kate's home. Another lovely cottage, but with the little extras that Maddy had thought that Ed's cottage lacked. This was a home.

Angie was waiting there. 'Take your dress off and stand in the middle of the floor, please,' she said.

Maddy did as she was told, standing still as the bronze silk was carefully lowered over her head. Angie walked round her, pulled at a sleeve, adjusted the hang at the back. 'Not bad,' she muttered. 'Just a bit of alteration.' Like all dressmakers she put pins in her mouth then started to take in here, let out there. And then eventually Maddy was told, 'Now you can turn and look at yourself.'

Kate had brought a full-length mirror into the room. Maddy did as she was told. And she thought she looked wonderful. The dress was simple, elegant. It brought out her figure and enhanced her colouring. But the bandages on her head spoiled the overall effect.

'I know what you're thinking,' Kate said. 'Don't. The bandages will go, your hair will grow again.'

Maddy smiled ruefully. 'I know. It's a truly gorgeous dress and the cut is absolutely wonderful.' She meant it. But she couldn't sound too enthusiastic. When would she need an evening dress? Never in the foreseeable future.

So the week passed and she continued to improve. Nick came in, said how pleased he was with her progress. But he didn't mention his job offer again and she wondered why.

The dressing on her head was now much less obvious and she could feel the faint itching that said that her hair was beginning to grow again. But she still felt a mess. Who could possibly fancy a woman with half her head shaved?

She now went out every afternoon or evening with Kate. Although there was a difference in ages, they had become firm friends. She thought that working with Kate would be fun. But that would mean working with Ed. And she couldn't do that. Not if they didn't… And she hadn't found a job she fancied either. What was she to do?

Then it was the night before Ed was due to come back. She was both dreading and looking forward to seeing him. She had missed him so much! But she had also decided that Ed could not be held to a promise that he had made so thoughtlessly. What could she say to him?

Kate picked her up later that evening. 'Your dress has arrived,' she said as they drove down into Penhally. 'I've been desperate to see you in it, so we'll have a fitting at once. Angie asked if she could have a photograph of you in it.'

'Not with my hair like this,' Maddy said.

The car slowed, and Kate turned off the engine. Maddy peered out of the window and blinked. 'This isn't your house,' she said, her voice rising. 'It's Ed's cottage. What are we doing here?'

'Slight chance of plan,' Kate said briskly. 'Not important. You're still going to try the dress on. Now, out you get.' She helped Maddy from the car.

'But it's Ed's cottage!' Then she noticed there was a light on inside. 'Is Ed in there?'

'Let's go and find out.' There was a conspiratorial smile on Kate's face.

Maddy was instantly suspicious. 'I'm being set up here, aren't I?'

'I'm your friend, Maddy! No way would I set you up!' Kate didn't knock on the door, just pushed it open and then pushed Maddy into the cottage. 'I forgot something,' Kate went on. 'I'll have to fetch it. I'll be back in a quarter of an hour.' And she was gone.

Maddy stood there and looked at Ed. He was dressed in a white T-shirt and dark blue chinos. She had missed him so much. She had spent most of the past week thinking about him, remembering him, visualising him and his body and his smile… Now she saw him and there was a slight shock. He was more wonderful than she had thought. She just couldn't move.

He came over to her, put his hands on her shoulders and drew her to him. Gently, tentatively, he kissed her on the lips. Maddy waited a moment. It was all she could do. Then she threw her arms round him, pulled him to her and gave him the kiss that she knew he wanted. And that she wanted to give.

After ageless minutes they parted and he led her to the couch. He put his arm round her shoulder, she leaned against his chest. It was so warm and comfortable there! As if it was meant to be.

'I should be angry with you,' she mumbled, 'angry with you and Kate. You tricked me. Right now I'm too happy to be angry but I might get angry later.' Then she shook her head. 'Why am I talking this rubbish? First, why are you back early?'

He shrugged. 'Tomorrow is the plenary session. That means that people talk, argue and get nothing except the pleasure of hearing their own voices. I decided I had much better things to do here. I didn't want to spend an extra day without you so I came home.'

He eased her head away from him, stared at her. 'I want to look at you. You look so much better. How do you feel?'

'I'm not fully well but I'm getting there.' Then she had to be honest. 'I'm better just for seeing you. But—'

He held up his hand. 'No need for buts. Just sit here with me and I'll hold you and kiss you.'

'Seems a good idea for now. But there will be buts.' She didn't know how it was possible. She felt both at peace with the world and excited by it. Certainly she was happy. Later there might be the need to talk, to make decisions, to suffer even. But not yet. Surely she was entitled to a few minutes of worry-free happiness?

It seemed a short quarter of an hour, but when a knock came at the door she glanced at the clock she saw that, in fact, it had been nearer half an hour.

'Better let her in,' said Ed, and stole one last kiss before going to the door.

Kate came into the room, clutching a large purple paper bag. 'Girl stuff,' she said to Ed. 'You wander off somewhere and wait. We'll call you when we need you. Did you get a mirror, like I asked you?'

He went to the side of the room, turned round a large sheet of wood propped against the wall. On the other side was a full-length mirror. 'I took the door off my wardrobe,' he said. 'If you want anything, I'll be in the kitchen.'

'And don't peek!' Kate called after him.

Getting the dress was very nice, Maddy supposed, and she had to try it on. But she'd rather just be with Ed. Still, a lot of time and work had gone into this. She pulled off the dress she was wearing and hoped Ed was not peeking. Her underwear was decidedly practical.

Kate stood behind her. She put her arms over her head. There was a rustling sound and then the fabric slipped over her head and downwards. When the dress was sitting loosely on her shoulders she looked down in amazement.

This was not the bronze silk she had ordered, tried on. This was a much lighter colour—ivory. What was happening? She felt Kate zip up the back, pull at the shoulders and waist. She heard her mumble that it really needed a slip—but for now it didn't look too bad.

There was a tremor in Kate's voice. 'Maddy, you can look at yourself now,' she said. 'Ed! Come on out.'

Ed came out of the kitchen and Maddy stared at herself in the mirror. This wasn't the bronze dress she had been measured and fitted for. This was an ivory dress in raw silk. She realised that it was exactly the same pattern as the bronze dress had been, and it fitted her just as well and it was just as…well, more beautiful. But this wasn't an evening dress, it looked like a… 'This is a wedding dress!' she burst out.

'Well, so it is,' said Kate. 'How strange.' She and Ed exchanged complicit glances.

Maddy felt… What did she feel? A maelstrom of emotions.

'You planned this between you!' she cried. 'You got me a wedding dress when I hadn't asked for one.'

'It wasn't Kate, it was all me,' said Ed quietly. 'It's all my fault. Kate had doubts—but I had hopes.'

'You got me a wedding dress! By deception!'

'True. Do you like it?'

She didn't know what to think, to feel. So in the end, after a long silence, she answered honestly, 'I couldn't think of anything more wonderful. If I was going to get married, that is.'

'Ah,' said Ed. 'Well, now we have to have a little talk.'

Maddy was still too dumbfounded to say anything. But

from behind her she heard Kate say, 'You know, I really want to stay here and listen. But reluctantly I'm going to go. Ed, you can take her back to the nursing-home later. Maddy, will you phone me some time tonight. Please?'

It seemed the smallest of her problems but she said, 'Who will help me out of this dress?'

'I will,' said Ed. 'It's something I've always wanted to do.'

'No,' Kate put in. 'This is a woman's job. Back into the kitchen for a moment.' As she unzipped Maddy she said, 'It works just as well in raw silk as in the other fabric, doesn't it? And I knew you liked ivory because you said so when we were watching Rowenna's wedding.'

'What about the bronze dress?'

'You've got that as well. For your next ball.'

Maddy thought it odd but she felt reluctant to take off this glorious ivory dress and put back on her rather ordinary blue one. But she needed to feel ordinary for a while. Still, she looked sadly at Kate who was carefully packing the dress back in the purple bag. 'Kate, I can't cope with all this. I don't know what I'm doing, whether to be blazing angry or tearfully happy. I just don't know.'

'That's your problem now. I'm out of things.' She kissed Maddy on the cheek. 'Just one bit of advice that life has taught me. If you find the man that you need, grab him at once. And don't forget my phone call. Bye!' And she was gone.

Ed came back into the room, carrying two mugs. 'I occupied myself by making us tea,' he said. 'I couldn't just stand still, I felt a bit…nervous about things.'

'So you should. Ed, how could you…? Why did you…? It's a wedding dress. Why a wedding dress?'

'It was my idea. I was talking to Kate on the phone and she told me about the evening dress. I thought, if one dress—why not two? Kate told me how you liked the colour ivory and how you liked raw silk. And about the style looking so good on you. Kate was doubtful but I persuaded her. I commissioned an extra dress. A wedding dress.'

'Just in case I needed it?'

'In case you needed it. And I'm afraid there's more.'

'More? How could there be? What more?'

'Let's start with one thing. You said you loved me?'

Maddy felt she was being drawn into something. But she found that she didn't really mind. Just where was Ed taking her? She answered his question honestly. 'Yes, I did say I loved you. Mind you, I thought I might be going to die. It does make a difference.' But after an internal struggle she told him the absolute truth. 'I still do love you.'

'Good. And I told you I loved you and I wanted to marry you. But you thought I might have changed my mind. You thought I had said it in a moment of high emotion and I might want to rethink it. You thought I felt trapped. Right?'

Well, it was sort of what she'd thought. 'I thought you might feel trapped,' she agreed.

He grinned, then leaned over her and kissed her. When he took hold of her hands she could feel the tension there. 'Maddy, I told you there was more. The more is…I trapped you back. I've got you a wedding dress. I know the groom isn't supposed to see the bride's dress until the ceremony but I decided to ignore that. I was breaking lots of other rules.'

From his pocket he took out the little leather box that she remembered. 'Here's the engagement ring I offered you.' He put it on the table in front of her. 'In a moment I want you to put it on. I phoned the local vicar, he's a friend of mine. He's booked us the church for the very end of May. I've circulated the information to everyone who knows us and told them to keep the date free.'

He smiled, but she could tell that there was hope and fear as well as confidence there. 'Maddy, you have to marry me. All the arrangements are made. You're trapped just as you imagine I was trapped. And we do love each other so much.'

He opened the little leather box, took out the ring and offered it to her. 'Will you marry me, Maddy Granger?'

She still hesitated. Could she marry a man like this? A man so determined? Then she saw the depth of his love in his eyes, an emotion that matched her own. 'Of course I'll marry you,' she whispered softly, reaching out a hand to stroke his beloved face.

He placed the ring on her finger, then pulled her into his arms and kissed her, a kiss that seemed to last an eternity. When he finally broke the spell, Maddy whimpered in protest and snuggled deeper into his chest.

'I think Kate is waiting for your phone call, my love.' He smiled.

EPILOGUE

IT WAS a wonderful wedding. Even the weather was right, warm but not too hot. The bride wore an ivory raw silk dress. She wore a veil, her head was covered with a little cap. Few people realised how artfully her hair had been arranged to look entirely normal. After the ceremony three girls asked Maddy for the name of her dressmaker.

The groom wore his military uniform. Maddy had never asked him the name of the regiment he had been attached to. But in the scarlet tunic that had been worn before the Battle of Waterloo, he looked magnificent.

Kate was a fantastic matron of honour, and looked beautiful in a new outfit made by Angie. Holding her hand was little Robbie, this time in a page-boy outfit, looking as pleased as anything as Mrs Cowley looked on proudly from her pew. Unusually, the best man was the groom's father. Ed had asked Nick, who had been at first surprised and then quietly honoured. But, of course, he didn't say so.

And Captain Smith gave the bride away, dressed in his naval uniform.

The reception was wonderful too, on a pretty white yacht moored in the bay. There was a great meal, there were witty speeches—including one by the bride—and afterwards a dance and party. But the bride and groom left early for their honeymoon. No one knew where. Ed was a great organiser.

After the guests had waved goodbye to the couple they trooped back into the hall and the music started up again. Time to have a good time! To celebrate!

Kate and Nick stood side by side on the deck, away from the music and laughter for a moment. For some reason they didn't want to go straight back in. Kate felt happy, as if a job had been well done. She wanted to dance, but not just yet. It had been an exciting but an exhausting day.

'Walk with me for a minute,' she said to Nick. 'I'd like some fresh air. It's lovely to see so many friends together but I'd like five minutes' peace.'

'Good idea,' said Nick.

She took his arm as they strolled along the deck. 'Are you happy for them?' she asked. 'Or, better, do you think they will be happy?'

'I think they will,' said Nick, cautious as ever. 'Ed is my son, but surprisingly I don't know him all that well. I realize he's had problems. That stretch in Africa, losing his first wife—they could have scarred him for life. And I don't mean only physically. Maddy had problems, too. But I think they'll be good for each other. And you helped bring them together, Kate. I have to thank you for it.'

Kate smiled. 'They're a lovely couple and what little I could do to help, I was happy to do. And didn't they look gorgeous together?'

Nick smiled his customary guarded smile. 'They say that the bridesmaids mustn't look more glamorous than the bride. Well, as matron of honour in that pink dress, you came close. You look beautiful.'

Kate was shocked—and then delighted. This was not the reserved man she knew. 'Nick? A compliment? Are you feeling well?'

'Never better.' They paced a few more yards and then he said, 'I was remembering when we two were young. Teenagers together. We were happy then.'

Now Kate was apprehensive, even bewildered. This was forbidden ground. They never talked about their past. As they walked on she tried to take her hand from his arm and he took her hand, put it back where it had been.

'On the ship,' he said, 'when Ed had sent for you and I came aboard later, I was angry because I hadn't been consulted. However…I looked in your cabin when you were asleep. You looked just as you did when we were young. And I realized we can't keep ignoring what happened the night of the storm years ago. The guilt we both feel has been poisoning our relationship.'

Now Kate was upset. 'Nick, this is a happy day, don't spoil it. It's not the time to drag out old memories. We get on well enough now. Besides, we had an agreement never to talk about that night.'

'We never made an agreement!'

'We never needed to! It was there, it was obvious.'

He stopped, took hold of her other arm so they were facing each other. She could feel the tears in her eyes, knew that he could see them.

'Kate, that night we made love! Don't you think we need to talk?'

'Perhaps,' she said quietly. 'Not now—but soon.'

* * *

Maddy and Ed hadn't moved too far for their honeymoon. Both had travelled a lot, they didn't need to go to foreign parts. Now they were sitting on the balcony of a gorgeous boutique hotel, watching the sun go down over the sea. On the table between them was the traditional bottle of champagne.

'It was an amazing day,' Maddy sighed as Ed popped the cork and pale champagne fizzed into her glass. 'Everyone seemed to have a great time. I even saw Kate and your father dancing. They seemed to enjoy being together. Do you think they are happy, Ed?'

'I think perhaps they could be happier.' Ed said. 'If they could find out how.' He put down the champagne bottle and smiled at his wife. 'But are we happy, Mrs Tremayne?'

'Very happy, Mr Tremayne.' She held up her hand, admired the new gold ring next to the antique one. 'Everything is wonderful. Everybody is happy, but mostly you and me.'

'That's true,' Ed said as he bent to kiss his beautiful new bride. 'And I don't think I could be happier.'

BRIDES OF PENHALLY BAY

Medical™ is proud to welcome you to Penhally
Bay Surgery where you can meet the team led by
caring and commanding Dr Nick Tremayne.
For twelve months we will bring you an
emotional, tempting romance – devoted
doctors, single fathers, a sheikh surgeon,
royalty, blushing brides and miracle babies
that will warm your heart…

*Let us whisk you away to this Cornish coastal
town – to a place where hearts are made whole.*

Read on for a sneak preview from
Single Dad Seeks A Wife
by Melanie Milburne
– the seventh book in the
BRIDES OF PENHALLY BAY series.

SINGLE DAD SEEKS A WIFE
by Melanie Milburne

Eloise found the local police station without too much trouble, although when she opened the front door she was a little surprised there was no one seated at the small front desk. Penhally Bay was so quiet she could hardly believe it had a police station and certainly not one where a chief inspector had been appointed.

She looked over the counter to find a bell or buzzer to push, located a small brass bell and gave it a tinkle. She hovered for another minute or two before she called out, 'Hello? Is anyone there?'

No answer.

She gave the bell another rattle, feeling a little foolish as she did so. But then she had to admit she had never felt more ill prepared for a professional appointment in her life, let alone her first international assignment. It seemed ironic to have been so churned up with nerves only to find the station she had been assigned to work from was far from a high-tech law-enforcement agency.

She was glad now she hadn't wasted precious time trying to find somewhere to buy a new outfit. Somehow turning up in her well-worn jeans and close-fitting vest top with a cotton shirt over the top didn't seem quite so out of place now. Admittedly, there was a coffee stain on her top on her right breast, where the mid-air turbulence had caught both herself and the flight attendant off guard during dinner, and her jeans felt as if they could have stood up all by themselves. As for her face…well…what could she say about her face? At least it was clean—the scalding blast of hot water in the shower a short time ago had not only lifted off thirty-six hours of make-up but what felt like the first layer of skin as well. Her fine blonde hair hadn't appreciated the detergent-like guest-house shampoo, and without her radial brushes and high-wattage hairdryer it was now lying about her scalp like a straw helmet instead of her usual softly styled bob.

She whooshed out a breath and raised her hand to the first door she could find, but before she could place her knuckles on the wood the door suddenly opened and a tall, rock-hard figure cannoned right into her.

'Oh…sorry,' a dark-haired man said as he looked down at her, his strong hands coming down on her arms to hold her upright. 'I didn't realise you were standing there. Did I hurt you?'

Eloise blinked a couple of times, her heart doing a funny little stumbling movement in her chest.

She swallowed and gave herself a mental shake. She was dazed by the sudden contact, that's what it was.

Of course it was, she insisted firmly.

It had nothing to do with intelligent brown eyes the colour of whisky and it had absolutely nothing to do with the feel of male hands on her arms for the first time in…well, a very long time indeed.

'Um…I'm…er…fine….' she said hesitantly. 'I rang the bell

but no one answered. I was just about to knock when you opened the door.'

He gave her a smile that lifted the corners of his mouth, showing even white teeth, except for two on the bottom row that overlapped slightly, giving him a boyish look, even though Eloise calculated he had to be close to forty.

'I'm sorry the front desk is unattended,' he said. 'The constable on duty left on a call half an hour ago and the other constable is off sick. What can I do for you?'

Eloise ran her tongue over her lips in the sort of nervous, uncertain gesture she had thought she had long ago trained herself out of using, but without the armour of her clean-cut business suit and sensible shoes and carefully applied but understated make-up she suddenly felt like a shy teenager.

And it didn't help that he was *so* tall.

She decided she would definitely have to rethink the sensible shoes thing in future otherwise she would be seeing a physiotherapist weekly if she had to crane her neck to maintain eye contact with him all the time. He was six feet one or two at the very least, his shoulders were broad and his skin tanned, as if he made the most of the seaside environment.

'I'm Chief Inspector Lachlan D'Ancey,' he said offering her his hand.

Eloise's stomach did a complicated gymnastics routine as she blinked up at him in surprise.

He was the chief inspector?

Gill Sanderson

QUESTIONS & ANSWERS

Would you like to live in the fictional Cornish town of Penhally Bay?

Penhally Bay sounds a wonderful place to live. I'd love the walking, the sailing, the swimming. However, it's too far from anywhere to climb. The nearest mountain range I can find is the Black Mountains in South Wales. I need to be not more than an hour's drive from high places, so sadly Penhally Bay won't do.

Did you enjoy writing as part of the Brides of Penhally Bay series?

Very much so. At first I was worried; I was supplied with a background, characters, a story line and had to write within these constraints. Usually I like to create my own stories. However, after a time I found this not a problem. There was plenty of scope to work out my own ideas. And the feeling that I was not just writing my piece, but contributing to the thrust of a greater story – that was another bonus.

What was it like working with other authors to create the backdrop to these books?

It was great! Normally I send a synopsis to my editor, she comments on it and I then write the book according to what we agree. If there are any problems in writing the book, then I e-mail or phone her for her suggestions. But I have to remember she's the editor for a number of writers, I can't monopolise her attention. However, this book is one of a series of twelve. Nine writers, all with their own views on background, character (especially of Nick and Kate), on the progression of the overall story.

And I could get in touch with any of them! Suddenly, writing had become a group endeavour, which was something new to me. The one problem? What if they didn't like the brilliant idea I'd spent three days working on?

Tell us about a typical day's writing!

I'm a professional writer. I sit facing a computer screen with a blank wall behind that (the blank wall is important. Nothing should distract you). Five days a week I sit at my desk at half past eight in the morning and work through solidly until half past one. There is no waiting for inspiration, I just write. Of course, sometimes what I write is rubbish, but I don't stop. Soon enough the ideas will catch fire and when that happens there is no joy like it. For a couple of hours in the afternoon I go to the gym or for a run along the beach. Then it's a trip to a library to research or back to the study to amble round the internet in search of other material (very time-consuming). Just before I go to bed I read through what I have written in the day. This means that next morning ideas will come so much more easily.

What do you love most about your hero and heroine in _Nurse Bride, Bayside Wedding_?

I like characters who get on with their job no matter what their personal feelings are. Maddy and Nick both have demons – but those demons have to take second place to their work. I also like characters who see what they want and go for it.

Can we have a sneak preview of your next book…?

In the book I have just finished, a newly qualified doctor, city born and bred, comes to do a year's work in a small town in my much-loved Lakeland. She is quite attracted to the doctor who will mentor her but she daren't fall for him. He has a young son…